NO WAY OUT

Melanie Forbes

Acknowledgments

I would like to start off by thanking God for allowing me to even get to this point. Without Him and His grace and blessings, none of this would be possible.

Next, I would like to thank my mommy, Juanita Burroughs. You're the best mom ever. Thanks for everything. Love you to pieces. My sister, Tahirah Burroughs, thanks for being a great support system, always being there, and being the first to read my book. Rodney Butler, you're the best. Thanks for your advice and for pushing me in a positive direction. My BFF, Kiauna Bradshaw, thank you for always being there for me. You always have, and I know that you always will. Finally, thanks to Antoine "Inch" Thomas for answering all my questions and giving me so much helpful advice on my book.

There's a list of others. If I did not say your name, just know I'm thankful for everyone that's been there for me. I love you all. And to everyone that reads my book and shows support, I appreciate all of you. Just know this has been a very long and hard journey for me, but even when I felt like giving up, God gave me a reason to go all the way, and that's what I did. Again, thank you, Lord, for everything.

This book is in loving memory of my dad, my hero, Floyd Forbes. Love you always. You will forever be my angel.

Chapter One

Mmm... he was so fucking sexy. Caramel complexion, light brown eyes, pretty teeth, dimples, nice body, and a beautiful smile. I could go on and on, 'cause he was all that and a bag of chips. And with all the shit Shawn put me through, hell, I could use a new friend, anyway. This sexy, caramel thing named Jerimiah had just gotten a job at the Burger Café, a spot that I had been working at for a while. All of the bitches there wanted him, but I knew that I was going to fuck Jerimiah first.

Out of all of the girls working at the Burger Café, I stood out the most. My beautiful, chinky brown eyes got me the nickname Beauty. My real name was Mariah. The whole entire staff wanted me, even my manager, Mack.

Mack was a very attractive man, but he was also a married man. He was cool as shit, but he could be very irritating at times. Mack was in his forties, but he had a thing for young girls, especially me.

Anyway, the Burger Café used to hire recovering addicts. They were sort of giving

1

them a second chance or some shit. There were three main ones: Lauren, Alicia, and Kim. Lauren was a diabetic and would constantly have diabetic attacks while cursing someone out at the same damn time. But poor Ms. Lauren didn't mean nobody no harm.

The crazy thing about it was that we had a sixty-year-old faggot as our store manager. He was Mack's boss. He was mean as shit and literally hated women, whether they were pretty, slim, fat, or ugly. He didn't discriminate. When Ms. Lauren would have her attacks, Paul's faggot ass would always be there. She'd always appear to be fine when Paul wasn't at work.

Then, we had Alicia, the gangster crackhead. She used to rob and steal for a living. Last but not least was your girl Kim. There was talk around the job that she had AIDS. She wasn't that attractive either. She was missing some teeth, and the only thing shorty had going for her was that big-ass booty that drew a lot of attention her way.

Kim had had a very hard life. She'd told me many stories of her previous drug addiction, how she had been raped from her asshole, and how it kind of turned her on. She and Mack had begun to get close to the point where he'd get defensive if anyone even mentioned Kim. She was his new boo. Rumors spread that they were in a sexual relationship. I hoped not, for Mack's sake. Kim didn't last too much longer at the Burger Café.

No Way Out

Chapter Two

Alicia and Jerimiah were talking as I walked past, so me and Jerimiah began exchanging words with our eyes.

Alicia said, "Hey! Beauty, this is Jeri. He's new."

So, I introduced myself. It didn't take a rocket scientist to see that Alicia had the hots for Jeri.

But, I, being the bitch that I am, thought, *Fuck that crackhead-ass bitch!* She was old as fuck, anyway. Plus, she wasn't any competition compared to me.

I walked past him as he was cleaning up the store, and he smiled at me. I smiled back, and he asked me if I knew how to braid hair.

"Hell yeah," I said. "That's what I specialize in."

I knew how to get exactly what I wanted. I gave him my number with the hopes that he would call that same night, but he didn't. The very next day, I checked the schedule to see the next time that he worked, but when that day came, he never showed up.

No Way Out

When Jerimiah finally decided to show up for work, I asked him why didn't he call me. He just gave me some lame-ass excuse. Not to mention that he had a passion mark on his neck and made up this dumb-ass lie, saying that some chick was so pressed over him that she did that on some hating shit and that the only reason he was over her house was because he sold drugs for her Jamaican brother. I didn't believe that shit— not one bit— but I didn't really care, because he wasn't my man. I just went with the flow.

After all the small talk and games, Jeri finally decided to make his way to my house, where I stayed with my mom, stepdad, and god sister. Jeri and I chilled that night. At least, I did. Jeri had gotten excited, laying in the bed next to me while we watched TV. We kissed and hugged and then hugged and kissed, but nothing happened that night, even though I wanted it to. My mind wasn't really there.

I was an emotional wreck, and even though they called me Beauty, I didn't feel that way. I mean, I had been through hell. Jeri and I had been seeing each other for a while, but I still had feelings for my ex, Shawn. As much as I wanted to see Shawn, I started standing him up so often that he eventually left me alone for good. I couldn't lie; I was never really in love with Shawn. He was an ugly-ass nigga that would take me shopping and buy me everything that I

6

wanted. But, see, that was his game. He did that with all of the girls. That's how he baited us. Shawn always kept a good job and had lots of potential. He even went to acting school with hopes of pursuing a career in film, but his acting career didn't go far.

I always had big dreams of modeling and acting, and even a little rapping, but Shawn enhanced them. Shawn's drive for wanting more constantly motivated me to dream bigger. At the same time, I was scared to leave my hometown of Baltimore for long periods of time, because Baltimore was all that I really knew. It was my comfort zone.

Shawn was the type of dude that would sell a woman a dream and give her whatever she wanted, but best believe she went through a lot to get whatever she asked him for. Plus, the bullshit with finding out about other bitches leaving his home. Like, one time in particular, after I left the Burger Café, my intuition was kicking in overtime. I had called Shawn, and he wasn't answering his phone. Plus, he was supposed to be taking me shopping and out to eat the very next day. So, after work, I decided to listen to my sixth sense and do a little investigating of my own.

As I approached his house to knock on the door, I caught him in the car with this ugly bitch. I knocked on the girl's car window and asked him, "Who the fuck is she?"

He replied, "My friend!"

When he stepped out of the car, I took my fist and sucker punched the shit out of him. I was turned all the way up. I mean, I was heated. I turned around to walk across the street to my sister's apartment, and the stupid bitch kept on asking me was if everything was okay. I told her that hoe she could get what Shawn had gotten if she didn't mind her fucking business!

She left, and I went inside my sister's house. Shawn followed me in and kept on trying to grab me because he'd gotten caught cheating on me. I ended up breaking my sister's chair on his stupid ass by mistake because I was so angry. My sister tried to break it up. Of course, I paid her for the damages to her chair.

Chapter Three

You see, when I first met Jeri, I was emotionally unstable. I didn't even get a chance to have some alone time after the Shawn situation. Jeri would meet me at the Burger Café every day that I was scheduled to work. He still had a job there but he didn't work many hours. Crazy shit is that he barely came to work on the days he was scheduled to. He would bring me gifts such as, teddy bears and cards, and he took me shopping and stuff just like Shawn used to do. The week after we made everything official, Jeri took almost all of his clothes to my house and told me that he needed to stay a week because there was something going on at his house.

I just took his word for it. Something didn't seem right, but I didn't ask any questions. A week soon turned into a month, and my nagging-ass stepfather, Leroy, brought it to my mother's attention. She began complaining about Jeri coming over all the time, and Leroy complained about Jeri eating all of the food and not paying any bills.

No Way Out

Jeri was going a bit overboard on the eating tip, but I ignored the signs. Once I really got to know Jeri, I realized that he really had no place to go. And with us being around each other all day and night, he began to suffocate me to the point that I needed some to get away from him, at least for a little while.

I slowly started hanging around my friends less. Things had even started getting a little awkward between my god sister, Chanel, and I. We really wouldn't hang out as much, either. Then, my mother really started tripping, saying that she was tired of seeing his face every day when she came home from work and that he needed to go home sometimes. Sad thing is that I was starting to feel the same way. I was just too nice to people sometimes, and I didn't want to just leave my boyfriend homeless. I felt partially responsible.

I didn't want to admit it, but I honestly knew that I was wrong for letting Jeri stay there. At the time, I was still working at the Burger Café, and many of the employees knew that Jeri and I were together. Mack was one of the many people who didn't agree with our newfound relationship. Mack had a special name for Jeri. He called him Knucklehead. Mack had become extremely jealous to the point that it would interfere with us working together.

Mack would purposely curse Jeri out or find any reason to suspend him. He even tried to fire Jeri on several occasions.

One day, I was working in the drive-thru window, and Mack started yelling at me for no reason. He said it was because he was mad at the fact that Jeri was there. He claimed that we'd had a customer sitting at the window for a long time, so me and Mack got into it. Next thing I know, Jeri butted in and told Mack to stop fucking yelling at me. They began going back and forth, cursing each other out, then they got up in each other's faces, and Mack told Jeri that he could leave. I couldn't believe it! Mack actually called himself firing Jeri, but Paul was definitely not having that.

It had gotten to the point that, if I went in the freezer at the café to get French fries, nuggets, or whatever we needed, Mack would wind up in the freezer with me, trying to push up on me. One day, he told me that if I didn't give him a kiss, I couldn't go on my lunch break. Mack had really started pissing me off with the picking and the nagging like a bitch. It was the same old shit every day. It was bad enough that he was married and would tell me how he would leave his wife for me. I mean, this motherfucker even went to the extreme. He once told me that he wanted me to come over to their house and braid his hair.

11

That was some fucked up shit, and it was absolutely unacceptable. There was no way in hell I was going over there and putting myself in the middle of that bullshit. Apparently, his wife wasn't fucking his ass right, because he surely acted like he needed some pussy.

Now, Mr. Paul would stay on your ass. He didn't give a fuck who you were. He didn't back down from nobody. On top of that, he didn't know how to talk to people, but he took a personal interest in Jeri and this other dude named Tony. They would come to work late on a regular basis, and that was if they showed up at all. I used to joke with Jeri and tell him that Mr. Paul was his sugar daddy. Mack had already fired Jeri, but Paul's ass let him come right back to work.

Tony's girlfriend Tamia was not on Mr. Paul's list of favorite people, simply because she was dating Tony. If she even thought about being late to work, he would curse her ass out. He eventually wrote her up, and not long after that, he made up an excuse to fire her with the help of this Trinidadian bitch that came from another store to help us out.

Now, this bitch right here was jealous of all of the bitches and wanted all of our niggas. See, she was married, too, and her husband managed the store that she came from. Around her husband, she played so innocent, but everybody else knew that she was a hoe. Zalou was her name.

Zalou also wanted Jeri and Tony, but they were both occupied. As you know, Zalou didn't like me or Tamia, so Paul and Zalou set Tamia up to be fired. It was something about that bitch, Zalou, I never trusted, anyway. I told Tamia's ass not to trust that hoe. Too bad for her. Trust had become her downfall, because it got her ass fired.

No Way Out

Chapter Four

Jeri and I had been together for a few months, and I was starting to notice that all he wanted to do was drink. I mean, every day. It did not matter to him whether it was morning, noon, or night. He barely wanted to work or do anything for himself, for that matter. Sometimes when I would get off of work, I would get my homeboy, Richard, or his bro, Marvin, to take me home.

Richard and Marvin both liked me, but I knew Richard first. Richard was an old homeboy from way back in the day. Richard would come over and chill with me from time to time, but that was it. He was like my little drink and smoke buddy. Richard and I shared an open friendship. We'd spent a lot of time together through the years. Since I was sixteen years old, I'd thought about us being serious, but kind of in a joking way. But there was never nothing more than that.

Jeri sensed that Richard and Marvin liked me, but I lied to him and told him that they were my cousins and were just very playful at times. I knew that if he found out, he would flip the fuck out. Jeri had become verbally abusive to the point that I'd become depressed. Before Jeri came along, I had saved up a whole lot of money with plans of taking that big step and moving out of state to New York City, but Jeri had become so needy that I had started pinching off of my money here and there, not to mention that we both ended quitting the Burger Café.

Dealing with Mack and his faggot-ass boss, Paul, was beginning to be too much. Plus, when Elroy was there, you had to worry about your drawer coming up short. Elroy was a manager, too, but all his fat ass could manage was the food he was eating and the money he was stealing out of other people's cash registers.

All me and Jeri had was a whole bunch of time on our hands, because neither one of us had jobs anymore. Once we became unemployed, I really started noticing things about Jeri that I didn't like. He wouldn't clean up behind himself anymore. I noticed that he was always angry and that, if he wanted his way with me, he would use reverse psychology on me and compare me to his ex-girl, Martha. One day, he showed me a picture of Martha, and she wasn't even attractive. Her ugly ass looked like she belonged to somebody's jungle, but she had to be good for something, because he damn

16

sure had a homemade tattoo with her name on his arm that I hated to look at.

My mom was still bitching about Jeri, but the problem was that Jeri had become the main topic in my mother's home. Since I knew Jeri had nowhere to go, I had to think of a plan, because I couldn't just leave my man homeless. Even though Jeri was mean, I knew that he loved me very much, because he never wanted to leave my side. So, I thought of the perfect plan.

The big plan was to sneak him in the house and that would be a very difficult task, because my mom and stepfather would be there, not to mention the fact that Jeri had to eat. That would call for me being in my room more often with the door closed, which was so not me. I would call it suspicious behavior. So, I would fix myself a plate and add a little bit more for him. We would still be hungry, but at least we both got to eat.

Sometimes, Leroy could feel that Jeri was in my room hiding, so when he would come in at night, he would keep their room door open so that I couldn't sneak Jeri in the house. That still didn't stop me. At times, I would have Jeri hiding on the steps and, when Leroy and my mother weren't paying attention, I would make Jeri crawl past the room as I shielded his body, and then I would close my room door and sigh in relief. That would require us to talk very softly, because sometimes, Leroy would be listening out for his voice. Leroy enjoyed that type of shit, anyway. He loved himself some drama. Boy, oh, boy, that was his thing.

Chapter Five

After three-and-a-half to four months of being in a relationship with Jeri, I was pregnant. I had no idea until I missed my menstrual cycle. We didn't waste any time at all. I didn't want my mom to know that I was pregnant because I was such a private person. I guess it's safe to say I was shy. So, I started staying over my sister's house to hide it from everybody. I didn't even have enough strength to wash myself up. Luckily, Jeri happened to find a new job right away.

The crazy part about the whole pregnancy was that I brought myself a home test and it came up negative. But when the smells of certain foods started making me throw up, I decided to go to the hospital and get a blood test done there. Jeri could not believe that I was pregnant, but he wanted me to keep his baby. After being at my sister's house for so long, I had finally run out of clothes to wear, and I was a little too weak to go back to my mom's house to get myself some clean clothes.

No Way Out

My sister let me wear one of her long, white T-shirts to sleep in. Not long after, Jeri was on his way to work at about five o'clock in the morning, and he started this big argument because my sister's boyfriend was in the other room asleep and my T-shirt came up just a little, even though nobody was even in the room to see it. The nausea and vomiting made me sleep wildly because I was so sick.

He got so jealous even though nobody saw my shirt rise a little. And bickering back and forth for about half an hour, Jeri decided to do the unthinkable— he hit me. Not only did he hit me, he kept on doing it, knowing that I was pregnant. I had already lost so much weight from carrying the baby, so I didn't have enough energy to fight him off the way I normally would. I felt so bad that I couldn't defend my unborn child.

After he hit me for the last time, he dragged me off of the sofa, put me in the shower, and turned the water on while I still had my T-shirt on. My sister and her boyfriend woke up, and then we just got real quiet and pretended that nothing happened as usual. That wasn't the first-time Jeri pulled that stunt. He'd done it before at my mom's house. My god sister, Chanel, had come home from school and heard us fighting, so she kicked my bedroom door in, and then we kicked his punk ass. She'd been waiting to get her hands on him.

Knowing he was a man that was built different and much stronger than me, he took advantage, and he knew it. It seemed like he felt good about it, like it gave him power or control. It started from upstairs, and then we ended up downstairs. My god sis was not a small chick and she had a few mental issues, so she gave his ass a run for his money, and he didn't like that. Not one bit.

I was young, naïve, and had a lot to learn. This was like a nightmare. I couldn't believe that I, Beauty, could ever get abused by a man. I was supposed to be enjoying the pregnancy that Jeri and I had planned. The sad news was that I couldn't enjoy it because me being pregnant only made Jeri worst, and he had become very overprotective and too damn controlling. I thought I had two fathers for a second.

Jeri's mom, Trecy, was happy to find out about my pregnancy, and the fact that she was having a grandchild made everybody want to look past the abuse. After making it about five to six weeks into my pregnancy, I decided to get an abortion. I was tired of fighting, and I couldn't get past the abuse. Knowing how crazy Jeri was, I knew that he would have tried to take my child or something just to hurt me. I would have had to sacrifice my freedom, because I would have killed his ass. Jeri wasn't worth it. Not one bit.

No Way Out

So, there you have it. The pregnancy was terminated and, once Ms. Trecy found out, she didn't care too much for me anymore.

I had gotten so frail and skinny that you could literally see the skeleton in my face. I was so weak that I couldn't even stand up straight. My ribs were showing like an Ethiopian child's. It took weeks after the abortion for my body to get back to normal.

People began to notice a change in me, physically and mentally, and began to question what was going on with me and Jeri. After that whole ordeal, Jeri found every excuse in the book to put his hands on me. He would call me horrible names like stupid, freak, and worst of all, baby killer. He would try to put me down and tell me how all of his past girls had way more than me.

After the abortion, I ended up going back to my mom's house. It was time for a new start, so I started searching for a new job. The job search finally began, and I got the break that I needed: an interview at the Burger Café. This one was much closer to my mother's house, so I could walk there.

Once I started working there, the jealousy started all over again. One night, I had to work the overnight shift, and my manager, Tarsha, asked me if I needed a ride home, and I had to tell her 'no', even though I didn't really feel like walking home late at night after working for eight hours. But Jeri was going to meet me after work, and I knew that he wouldn't want to ride with them. Besides, I couldn't do anything without Jerimiah's permission, anyway.

I knew that I would have to ask him first, and, just like I'd thought, he didn't want the ride because he didn't want me to meet any new people. Jeri made us walk about ten long blocks in the freezing cold after midnight to get home, tired and all. It was late and below zero degrees, and his only concern was me not having any friends. We kept up with this routine for about three or four months, and then I finally got the chance to work the evening shift. This was the shift that I really wanted in the beginning. I just settled for the overnight shift to get my foot in the door.

No Way Out

Chapter Six

It was hard at first, trying to manage hiding all of the mental and physical abuse that I was dealing with, but I was able to do it for a while until Jeri started coming up to my job all the damn time. I mean, every fucking day that I worked, he made sure he was there. My coworkers started to sense all of the tension that was in the air. Jeri had a way of intimidating people with his looks. If looks could kill, there would have been a lot of dead motherfuckers.

As the months went on, he wasn't just mugging my coworkers. He went on to doing embarrassing shit to me at the job. I remember one incident in particular where we had an argument on the way to my job and Jeri snatched my wig off in front of my coworkers and choked me out in front of one of my managers. It wasn't like this was somebody cool. I'm talking about a big, fat, ugly, pink lip bitch, whose skin was as black as tar, who ran around telling everybody's business, started shit, and would make up lies on you.

I remember being so embarrassed that day. I had so many mixed emotions running through my head, because, now, everyone would know for sure. I knew they had a feeling, but with no proof, it meant nothing at all. And I now needed help from a girl I hated. She called the police on him. It didn't help because he was already gone, and I was standing there with my hair looking a mess and tears in my eyes, just looking so confused, wondering how could he do this in front of my coworkers. As usual, all he did was apologize and tell me the same old bullshit about how he would never do it again.

My manger, Tarsha, and I had become very close friends, and she had been through a similar situation in her relationship. One day, she approached me about it, and I confided in her and told her the truth because, for some reason, I felt like I could trust her. Besides, the other manager, better known as Blacky, told everybody what happened, but she switched the story up so bad, you would have thought I had to go to the hospital for weeks.

I took off of work for a few days and decided to spend the weekend with my mommy and clear my head. Me, my mother, and my stepfather, Leroy, decided to head out to Laurel, MD and visit my auntie Janet and maybe do a little shopping. We hung out with them for a while and ended up going over Aunt Janet's house so that my cousin, Julia, could do my mom's hair. On a normal day, I was my mom's main hairstylist, but Julia was good with natural hair.

While we were gone, Jeri was at the house all alone, doing Lord knows what. He was such a sneaky motherfucker. The whole time we were gone, I was fucking paranoid. The plan was for Jeri to stay in my room until I got back home, and I would call home so that he would know to get back in the closet for hiding so we wouldn't get caught. Well, everything was going as planned until I got the strangest feeling, so I went along with my instinct and picked up the telephone and redialed the last three numbers on my phone while Jeri was hiding.

I found a number with star-sixty-seven directly in front the numbers. The first thing that came to my mind was, *I know this sorry-ass, homeless motherfucker isn't calling any bitches on my phone.* So, curiosity killed the cat and I did what any average bitch would have done. I called the number back. No one answered, and my heart dropped right into my shoes. The anticipation was killing me.

Just as I suspected, I heard a female's voicemail! All I could do was pace back and forth as I contemplated what I was going to tell her. Instead of leaving her a message, I called her back. I mean, I wanted some answers, so I left Jeri's ass upstairs, cramped up in that little-ass closet.

27

I went back down to my mother's basement to call this bitch, and she finally answered her cell phone. She had some explaining to do, and I meant business.

"Who this?" she asked. "I'ma have to call you right back because I'm at work."

I said, "Well, this is Jeri's girl. I'ma need to know what's your business with him."

"Well, he's chilled with me a few times, and he told me that you're a crazy bitch. Please don't call my phone anymore."

While I'm talking to her on the phone, this motherfucker was all the way upstairs, stomping on the fucking floor making hella noise, knowing that Leroy was upstairs wide awake. I guess that was Jeri's way of forcing me to come back upstairs since he didn't know what I was doing or what I could have been up to.

The phone was silent for a second, and then I asked her if she worked at his job, and she admitted that she did. We both got quiet again for another brief moment, and then I told that bitch, Shaunte, "Well, Jeri warned you for a reason, so if you know like I know, you would want to leave him alone before I come up to your job and fuck you up."

Jeri had started working at a nursing home in the dietary field and had been cheating on me with Shaunte, the bitch on his job. Even though she said that they hadn't had sex yet, he was getting very close to her, spending lots of time,

28

and most importantly, talking to this bitch on my house phone. For the life of me, I couldn't figure out what this stupid motherfucker could have been thinking since he didn't have anywhere to live.

Meanwhile, his dumb ass was still upstairs in my room with the door closed. I had him up there for a very long time. I called myself trying to be smart, but my actions caused Jeri to be even smarter.

I guess I must have pissed him off because he didn't know what was taking me so long, and that drove him crazy, but even more so because he was getting very cramped up from sitting in that closet balled up for about two hours straight. So, to make me come back upstairs into my room, Jeri did the stupidest thing that he could, and that was to start stomping. Not just any stomping. He was stomping very loudly and Leroy was wide awake in the room that he and my mom shared right next door to mine, sitting right at the computer playing solitaire.

I could hear Jeri stomping, and I was all the way in the basement. He was two whole floors above me. I panicked, hoping that Leroy didn't hear him and, just when I calmed down, Jeri did it again.

That's when Leroy asked my mother, "What was that noise?" with bass in his voice.

It was all over. We were caught red-handed.

No Way Out

My mother flipped the fuck out, and Leroy called the police on Jeri. And to top it all off, Jeri had come out from hiding in the closet and gotten in my bed butt-ass naked. My mother told Jeri that he had to get the fuck out, and since I wanted to be with him so bad, she told me to leave, too. I knew I had fucked up big time. I had lost my mom's trust, and now, I was going to be homeless just like this piece of shit that created all of these problems. That's what he wanted, anyway.

Shortly after all of the bickering back and forth amongst Jeri and Leroy, the cops finally arrived. Once they came inside of the house, my mom and Leroy told the police everything that happened, and then she asked me to leave, too. It was so fucking embarrassing. I was crushed.

I felt the tears coming, but I held them back as much as possible and tried to suck it up like a big girl. The officers started throwing slurs at me. I guess they sort of felt sorry for my mom or some shit like that. I'm not really sure, but that female cop started with the wrong bitch. Me and the cop started to argue, and I remember telling her that the only reason she was over there running her mouth was because she had that fucking gun on her hip.

"Beauty, shut up! Just shut the fuck up before they lock your stupid ass up!" Leroy yelled.

I did just that and gathered a few items, and then Jeri and I left, unsure of where we were going to go. We only had about thirty dollars to our names, and that was between the both of us. We didn't have too many places to go because no one could stand Jeri, not even his own fucking family. And, even though all of this shit was his fault, I wouldn't dare leave my man with nowhere to go. If I didn't help, I knew that another bitch would, and I kind of felt like it was my responsibility.

We went to 7-11 and got ourselves two hot dogs a piece. Mine had chili and mustard. I remember it like it was yesterday. I also got an ice-cold Pepsi and a cookies and cream candy bar. All of that food, and we still had to find a place for us to go and eat it.

We caught the subway, got off at a random apartment building, and pretended like we were waiting for somebody to come out. Once it got really late, we finally got comfortable and laid down In the hallway to get some sleep. It wasn't very cozy— the steps were pretty hard, the hallway was cold, and the residents were coming in and out all night. Sleeping in the hallway of an apartment building with strangers was scary since we didn't know who was who.

I remember thinking, *What if somebody hurts me, or what if people know that we're homeless and don't have any place to go?* But we made the best of our night and went to sleep.

I heard footsteps, and they got closer and closer. I finally opened my eyes, thinking I was dreaming, and there were two big, black men standing next to me and Jeri. I pretended that I was asleep as I watched the men, who had a big rifle pointed at Jeri's coat. I tried to dig in my pocket quietly to get my knife.

One of the guys turned around and looked at me. "What do we have here?" he asked. The guy grabbed me by my jacket, pulled me close to him, and licked my face. His breath smelled horrible.

Jeri yelled, "Let her go!"

The two men looked at each other and laughed. One guy kept staring at Jeri with this crazy look on his face and the rifle in his hand. The other guy grabbed me by my hair and began dragging me down the steps.

"The princess is going with me," he blurted.

"No!" Jeri screamed, though there was nothing he could at that point.

Crying, I yelled, "Jeri, please don't let him hurt me!"

The man dragged me down the hall and took me to a vacant apartment building. I kicked and tried to fight back, but he was just too big and much too strong. Once we got in the vacant building, he pulled a rusty, old knife out of his pocket and began to pop the buttons on my shirt.

"You don't want me," I said, "because I have AIDS."

With a chuckle, he said, "You're not saying nothing, lil mama. Me too."

It didn't work. My heart was racing as I tried to distract him so I could get the knife out of my pocket. At that time, the door opened.

It was Jeri standing there with the rifle, yelling, "Let her go before I splatter your brains all over the wall like I did your partner, nigga!"

The man laughed and said, "How can you to kill me when I'm dead already?" He took his hand a smacked me so hard that one could see the blood fly across the room.

I went to wipe my nose, and that's when I heard this *boom, boom, and boom.* The man went down right before my eyes.

Jeri ran over to me and gave me a great, big hug. I was so scared that I was shaking and crying at the same time. He took off his T-shirt and used it to clean the rifle, and then we got the hell out of there. We both swore not to ever speak on what happened to anybody.

No Way Out

Chapter Seven

Eventually, my mother let me come back home to stay. On one of my days off, I called up Toya, Leroy's niece, and told her that me and Jeri wanted to come over and hang out with her and her baby's father. Toya didn't mind because she had just gotten her own place and probably didn't mind the company, anyway. That gave us the chance to get a little bit of alone time in, being that my mom's house was too hot for Jeri to even be seen there.

So, we were over Toya's house, just sitting around, eating, talking, chilling, and watching scary movies. We were having so much fun. I smoked two blunts while they drunk some Goose, and then it started getting late, so we made a pallet on her living room floor. Toya and her baby's father, Dante, and their son, Jr., went into their room and closed the door. While they put their son to sleep, me and Jeri just laid there talking. About forty-five minutes later, we heard Toya moaning and groaning and calling for Dante. I could tell that he must have been putting in some work, because Toya sounded like she was really enjoying herself. All I could hear was, "Dante... Dante, please don't stop!"

"You love this dick, don't you?" Dante asked. "Whose pussy, is it?"

"It's yours and only yours, Dante. Just don't stop!"

Now, why did they give Jeri this crazy-ass idea that I wanted his ass touching on me? It was sickening to have Jeri touching all over my body and kissing all over my sweet places. Jeri was forcing himself on me, and I was softly pushing him away. I didn't want to fight Jeri; we'd had a good day. Besides, my pussy was so dry that I couldn't get wet if my life depended on it, but on a normal day, I would be wet as a river. It was just that Jeri had done so much to me that it was like he'd permanently turned me off. Even though he had saved my life, I think we were too far gone to even think about looking back.

Out of nowhere, my true feelings came out, and I whispered to Jeri that I was bored. This was while Jeri was licking on my stomach, and to make it worse, I said, "Wow, sounds like they're having so much fun in there."

Why did I have to start Jeri up, knowing that he had been drinking and how prideful he was? That quickly set him off. Jeri aggressively grabbed my clothes, grabbed me by my hair, and forced himself inside of me. He stroked about four times, and I wouldn't stop kicking and trying to push him off of me, so he covered my mouth.

He whispered in my ear, "I saved your life, so if you won't give me some pussy, I will take your life because I own you, bitch." He then tried to dig his fingers into my eyes while squeezing my mouth and noise shut so that I couldn't breathe.

I was petrified. I had to think of something quick. He took his fist and bashed me as hard as he could in my jaw. I thought he'd broken my shit. He tried to choke me, and I started feeling so lightheaded that I almost wanted to let myself go at that point. I was tired of fighting.

"I should kill you, bitch," Jeri said.

In my heart, I truly believed that that's exactly what he wanted to do. A part of me wanted to go, but I was too young to die from domestic violence. I honestly did believe that, one day, he really just might do it. So, I had no other choice but to scream as loud as I could. I used what little energy that I had left to scream Toya's name.

I kept yelling, "Toya, Toya, come help me please!"

That really made Jeri go crazy. He started choking me again and beating my head on the floor. He was kicking and biting me, too. I had so many bite marks on my body from Jeri that you would have thought that he was a cannibal.

No Way Out

As I started to drift away, Toya finally came out of the room. I was shaken up and my face was all swollen. There was no denying what Jeri had done. It was written all over my face, and I had the bloodshot eyes to match. Toya approached Jeri about what he had done., and he went off on her like he had something to prove. He didn't care at all that he was in this poor girl's house, in front of her son, acting like a maniac.

She wanted him to leave, and my scared, confused, embarrassed ass left with the very person that created all of this drama in the first place. This was cycle that kept repeating itself. Though I didn't want to tell my mother, I knew that Toya would tell her. See, the thing was, I wanted Jeri to stop whipping on my ass, but I wasn't ready to leave him alone.

Once we left Toya's house, we jumped right on the MTA bus and rode for several hours, trying to figure out what our next move would be. We didn't have a specific destination at all. We just knew that we wanted to be together at all costs. While riding the bus, I received several phone calls from my mother, father, and sister. They were very persistent about making sure that little old Beauty was okay. Little did we know, they were on a massive man hunt for Jeri's ass. They started as soon as Toya called them at about six o'clock in the morning with metal bats and all kinds of weapons and shit.

They were hoping to catch up to him and whip his black ass. Everybody that knew my dad knew that he kept a tool on him, so Jeri's ass was in hot water. He wasn't about to let no nigga beat on his baby girl. Plus, Toya lived in a very bad neighborhood with a terrible reputation. We had to walk through those projects at odd hours of the night. We had gotten tired of riding the bus all around the city, so I came up with the stupid idea to go to a cheap hotel so that we would have a chance to clear our minds our minds and figure the next move.

No Way Out

Chapter Eight

We finally made it to a cheap hotel called the Econolodge. It was a mini getaway, all expenses on me. When we first got there, Jeri and I looked around, and the bathroom wasn't very clean. The hotel had a little stench, and it wasn't what I was used to but it would have to do. Being that we were in an empty room with absolutely no cable and no entertainment, we decided to go outside and find some.

The first stop was right across the street from the hotel at McDonald's. We decided to go there. After all of the bullshit, I had worked up a big appetite. The next two stops were a bar and a clothing store, because we didn't get a chance to stop and get a change of clothes. Once we were done, we headed back to the hotel to get the young night started. We got a big-ass bottle of Ciroc with cranberry juice and a bottle of Moet, and before I knew it, I was fucked up. Everything seemed cool, and I had gotten very horny.

I couldn't even lie— the liquor had gotten the best of me, and I was down with whatever. I was ready to fuck. My pussy was wetter than a motherfucker. I had on some boy shorts, so my ass was looking kind of fat. In a see-through push-up bra, my thirty-eight C's were sitting nice and perky, and Jeri was looking and liking. I called myself teasing him and laid on my side and placed my ass on his dick. Jeri had gotten very aroused; his dick was so hard that he started pre-coming.

I suddenly felt his fingers between my legs as he moved my boy shorts to the side. When he felt my wetness, he really got excited. Next thing I know, he was finger-fucking me, and I was fucking his finger back. All of a sudden, he was sucking all of my sweet juices. We were so fucked up that neither one of us remembered if we fucked or not.

Day two, we got up, ate breakfast, and planned to do everything all over again. I stayed at the nasty store. They had so much lingerie that I liked. I was trying to get a nut. Me and Jeri had been beefing so much that I wasn't receiving the sexual attention that my body was craving. I bought a whip, some whipped cream, hand cuffs, and a kinky police officer outfit. We went back to the bar to buy a fifth of Ciroc and got tore up again. This time, I began to notice that Jeri was getting very aggressive, and he started getting on my damn nerves. He was trying to control my money. He wanted me to pay for everything— food, hotel, liquor, his cigarettes, and whatever else he wanted, along with our transportation.

My money was dwindling down drastically, and I was getting a little irked. Once he started drinking, he kept finding any little thing to argue about. The kicker was when my best friend Kia called my cell phone. Jeri instantly got jealous. Kia and I were tighter than glue. I was the godmother of all three of her children. Because I was giving Kia more attention than Jeri, he got mad and hung up the telephone on her. Next, he tossed my cell phone across the room.

I was drunk, angry, and ready to go the fuck home. I began to put my clothes on, and he got mad at me and pushed me to the bed. I waited for Jeri to go to the bathroom, and that's when I saw the best opportunity to run. By me not being able to run fast, I had to think fast and smart, so I ran to the side of the building. I saw Jeri when he came outside of the hotel looking for me. I was in the bushes, desperate to get away from him. With fear and tears in my eyes, I knew that I had no other choice but to make it to my mom's house. I would rather have her curse me out about the incident at Toya's house than to be caught by that drunken monster.

I saw a cab driver at the front entrance of the hotel, and he saw me hiding from Jeri. I pleaded with him just to take me all the way down the street, and he did just that. I wished I had enough money for the cab to take me all the

43

way to my mom's, but messing around with Jeri, all I had left was enough money to get on an MTA bus, and it was late, so the buses ran very slowly. Jeri would have caught me all alone. It was like he was a dog on my trail.

He caught up with me quickly, and I didn't understand how. Jeri saw that I was hiding behind a vehicle, and he jumped out of nowhere. I was so scared that I jumped in front of moving vehicle just to get away from him. I was screaming and dodging cars. I just knew that I was going to get hit, running for dear life. I was praying for God to just give me one more chance.

Finally, a car stopped. I screamed, "He's trying to kill me! Please take me to my mommy!"

The driver did so/ I couldn't stop crying. I was getting fed up. The nice guy got me home safely, and I offered him my last four dollars. He told me that he was a man of God and was an angel sent to help me and that he refused to take any money from me.

I thanked him again and went inside the house. I was just grateful to be home, away from that psycho.

Chapter Nine

Of course, my mom bitched, bitched, and bitched for about two weeks straight, threatening to whip Jeri's ass. To be perfectly honest, I would have actually been cool with that. In the middle of a conversation about Jeri, he had the fucking nerve to call my phone like nothing fucking happened and even had the audacity to tell me how he stayed at the hotel that Id paid for that night. I was pretty sure his bum ass probably got laid in there after telling some trick he had a hotel room. Just thinking about it pissed me off.

I stopped talking to him for a few weeks because I really needed a break, but, of course, I let Jeri's bum ass back into my life again. Meanwhile, Jeri had nowhere else to go, and I refused to let Jeri stay another night at my mom's house and risk me getting put out and being homeless too. I talked Jeri into asking his mother, Trecy, if he could stay with her for a little while until he got on his feet. At first, she refused. She was not feeling that because she was too busy kissing her husband's ass. Plus, she knew that her son was a loser and he had no intentions of doing anything better with his life. I guess that's where Jeri had got that shit from, because he told me how different guys would beat on his mom, and when he would try to defend her, she would only get mad and put him out of her house, so at an early age, he was out on the street messing with older woman just for a place to stay.

Finally, after all the begging, pleading, lying, and crying, Jeri finally convinced his mother to allow him to stay there, but it was under her conditions only. He didn't have a television to watch, and he could only use her house phone sometimes. He had restrictions on how much food could eat. It was almost like he was an orphan and not her first-born child. No one would ever allow Jeri to stay with them for long, and I mean no one, because Jeri didn't like rules, bills, respect, and not being in control of all situations at all times.

One day, he reached his breaking point and felt that he needed to take his control back. Since there was no television out in the living room where Jeri slept at night, he went and nicely asked Trecy if it was okay for him to borrow his little sister's TV for a little while since she was at school.

His mom shouted, "No!"

Jeri was furious at how petty his mother was acting, so he did what he did best: he blew the fuck up on everybody. He cursed his mother out so bad, calling her all types of bitches and shit. They went back and forth calling each other names— shit I would never say to my mother, personally. It was crazy. He brought out their ugly, dark past. She broke, even though she was being petty to begin with. I felt sorry for her.

In a soft-spoken voice, Mrs. Trecy told Jeri to get out, and I pleaded with Jeri to apologize and make things right. He swore that he knew everything and, even though his mother was wrong for how she handled things with her first-born child, he couldn't even hold his composure long enough to have a decent place to stay. Luckily, they had a storage room in his mother's building, and Trecy allowed Jeri to keep his clothing in there, because there wasn't enough room in her apartment to store Jeri's items. She even gave him the key.

What his mother didn't know was that once she put him out, he would still be sneaking in it. We went in there to lay down and tried to get us some rest. He used some of his blankets and put them on the hard floor so that we could try to get comfortable. Even with the blankets, it was hard to get comfortable because the floor was entirely too hard and cold. The storage room was very small and other tenants had keys to the storage room as well, which meant that we had to remain quiet at all times.

Jeri began to get agitated with me because he was so frustrated by the fact he didn't have anywhere to go. He took it out on me, almost as if he envied me.

I had very bad back problems, and I was getting tired of laying on that hard-ass floor. After turning so many different ways, you eventually run out of sides to turn on. I told Jeri that I was getting ready to leave and that I would holler at him the next day. The look on his face told me that I'd come face-to-face with the devil himself.

Jeri punched me so hard in my head that I literally saw lights flash. I knew instantly that I had to come up with a plan to get away from that crazy motherfucker. I mean, Jeri put himself in that situation and was actually blaming me for it. It was no one else's fault that he didn't want to follow the rules or that he didn't want to work. I mean, shit, most niggas were at least driving at his age.

To make a long story short, I told Jeri that I had to piss. That was my excuse to get outside so that I could at least get around some people. I couldn't believe that he would think I would have wanted to stay around him and chill with him after he just socked the shit out of me. I had used that excuse quite often, and he always fell for it. Once we got outside, I ran like a bat out of hell, screaming at the top of my lungs, "Somebody help me!"

By the grace of God, I saw a yellow cab sitting there like the driver was waiting on a fare. I pulled the door open and jumped in while yelling at the driver, "Please pull off. He's trying to kill me. Hurry up and pull off!"

The cab driver wouldn't listen, and Jeri jumped into the taxi with us.

With no other options left, I tried to call the police on my cell phone. As they answered, Jeri snatched my phone out of my hand and cracked me over my head with it. He was grabbing and pulling all over my hair, and he just wouldn't stop.

The cab driver remained in the same spot and was yelling for both of us to get out of his taxi. I began crying to him that if I got out of this cab, I was afraid that Jeri would kill me. The cab driver did not give a damn. I couldn't believe this dumb-ass cab driver was still running his meter and had the nerve to call the police on us, talking some bullshit about how we were going to pay him for his time. I told him to go ahead and call because, when I called the police, Jeri had hung up on them, and I needed some help. Besides, I had already figured that they wasn't going be hearing that shit. Anyway, once Jeri figured that the police were on their way, he ran off. I remained seated in the cab, patiently waiting.

Once the police arrived on the scene and listened to both sides, they began to curse the taxi driver out, telling him that he should have known better. The cab driver was still yelling that I owed him money. The officer turned around, said that I could have been his daughter who was getting beat up on, and told him to beat it.

Meanwhile, Jeri was out running around loose somewhere hiding, watching us somewhere very close by. The crazy part about it was that he had my shoes. He only took them so that I couldn't get very far. The police officer gave me a ride out of the wooded area even though they weren't supposed to do that. Once we got on a main road, they dropped me off. I knew that I had a head start away from Jeri, but I didn't know where Jeri was or what he was going to do since the police were called on him.

By that time, it was three o'clock in the morning, and it was hot as shit outside because it was summer time. I was just a young, black female walking late at night all by myself in Baltimore city's streets, trying to make it to my mom's house safely. Not only did Jeri take my shoes, but that bitch-ass nigga had also taken my phone and my purse, which had my house keys in it. How in the hell was I supposed to get in the house at that time of night? I knew that my mom would be in her room, asleep with the door closed and her television up loud.

As I waked home, I saw different men walking around looking suspicious, so I panicked, thinking they were going to try and hurt me. Because of Jeri, I didn't really trust men anymore. I thought that all men wanted to hurt woman in any way possible just because.

After about two-and-a-half hours of walking with no shoes on and the rocks and glass hurting and cutting my feet, I finally made it home, but it wasn't over yet. With all of this anxiety I had built up, I felt like I was going to pass out. My head was throbbing, and I felt a little knot on it. Once I got to the door, I had to forget about all that had happened and try to play it cool so that my mother wouldn't notice that anything was wrong with me. I knocked on the door as hard as I could while yelling my mother's name. Sadly, there wasn't a soul in sight, and every time I would scream for her, my voice would instantly disappear from all that yelling.

I sat outside for about forty-five minutes before my mom opened up the door. I had cried my little eyes out. I tried to hide it from her because she would have had a fit.

"Beauty, where in the hell is your keys and your shoes?"

I had to think of something fast, because my momma wasn't a fool. I told her that I had made a mistake and left the keys at a friend's house and that one of my flip flops had popped, so I just tossed the other one. She gave me a little look, but I was glad that she was too tired to fuss, because I was too. Plus, it was pretty late, so she just went upstairs into her room and went to sleep.

I did what I thought was best and took my tired, beat up ass to sleep.

The very next day, Jeri talked me into hooking up with his ass again. He called himself apologizing, and I fell for it. We went to his cousin's daughter's first birthday party. We appeared to be so happy. No one would have known what just had happened the night before.

Chapter Ten

Later on that evening, after the birthday party, Jeri decided that we should have a romantic evening at the downtown inner harbor. I was wondering how our day would go, but I had decided not to think too much about it. Besides, lately, good days were too hard to come by. I changed my clothing, did my hair, and got real pretty. Before I left the house, something told me to take a knife with me and put it in my bag, so that's exactly what I did.

Once we got down the inner harbor. we ate at Phillips Seafood and held hands, walking past the beautiful waterfront. It was a very beautiful night out. We decided to go and have a seat on a bench and discuss our problems. I thought that was a great idea. While talking, Jeri would not admit to his faults, and the conversation instantly went sour. He ruined my mood, and I was ready to go home. Jeri didn't want me to leave him, so he snatched my purse.

While he was running, I yelled out to him that I was going to call the police on him and within five minutes, we heard sirens passing, so

Jeri automatically assumed that I called the boys on him. So he got low, real low. I had no idea on where he had gone and that meant I was fucked. I had no money and no bus pass, so I had to fucking walk, and the sad part was that I had just gotten my purse back from him that day.

By me not really knowing my way around downtown like that, I decided to just walk to my sister's house because it was a much shorter walk. I really didn't know where I was going, but the neighborhood looked familiar. Those were the same projects where Toya lived at, and I was all alone. There were lots of dudes just sitting on their steps. There was a whole bunch of abandoned houses and those dudes were very loud.

One of the dudes yelled, "Aye, shorty, can I get your number, sexy?"

With a low, shy voice, I said, "I'm sorry. I have a boyfriend."

Out of nowhere, his homeboy started laughing and teasing the boy, saying that I had dissed him. I didn't understand why they thought I was being rude or lying, for the matter. Either way, homeboy was pissed off, and he started calling all of these females very loudly. I knew that whatever he called himself doing, it didn't sound good. I tried to walk a little faster, and next thing I know, I walked past two guys and overheard them saying something about how a girl was going to get fucked up.

I was mad, but my pride would not let me run. That thought never crossed my mind. Once I got to the main street, the whole neighborhood was outside for little old me. I decided to slow down, and then two big bitches walked up to me. One of the girls asked me if I had gotten smart with her brother, and that's when the other girl said something about her sister's boyfriend saying that I had gotten smart with him.

By that time, I was tired of being interrogated, because I already knew their purpose was to start some shit. I mean, that's what project bitches do. I just popped one of them and, after that, about ten bitches jumped on me. Niggas was standing around watching them attack me as if it was a football game or some shit. Luckily, a car riding past suddenly stopped. It must have been God.

In the car were a young, pregnant girl and her boyfriend. Once they stopped, the girls got off of me. I guess they were making sure it wasn't the police. The nice couple told me to get in the car, and I did. Once I got in, they made a U-turn in the middle of the street. Once we got to the light at the corner, I could hear and see one of the yo boys yelling and pointing in our direction.

The girl's boyfriend rolled down his window and told the little dude, "Yeah, you're right. We're over here. Would you like to get your little ass burnt up message boy?"

I guess homeboy didn't, because he surely did ride off down the street on his little bike. The driver let off two warning shots into the air as we were driving past. I knew that the driver was 'bout that life. He showed me his gun and told me that I was safe with them and that if his girl wasn't pregnant, he would have toasted them niggas. He tucked his gun back under his seat and proceeded to take me to my sister's house.

Once they dropped me off to my sister's complex, I saw the police, and I felt like telling them what had happened to me and what Jeri did too, but they were too busy harassing the niggas 'round the way, so I decided to just keep my mouth closed.

I knocked on my sister's door. My sister was a very hard sleeper, but I was determined to get in the house. After calling so many times, I almost gave up, and that's when my nephew finally opened the door, and I just broke down and started crying. I was so hurt.

After watching me break down like that, he went into his mother's room and tried to wake her up. It didn't work. I had a black eye, my lip was swollen, and my back was hurting, not to mention that I was limping. I didn't realize that I had been stabbed until my nephew started crying and saying that I was bleeding. I needed medical attention badly, but, instead of going to the hospital, I just decided to deal with it on my own.

I told my nephew to go back to sleep and that I would be okay. I limped into the bathroom, trying to get him off of me because I was losing so much blood. My nephew and I were very close. He could tell I was more hurt than I would admit. I convinced him that everything was okay, so he went to bed, and I closed the bathroom door, went into the cabinet underneath the sink, grabbed several towels, and applied them to my wound.

I freaked out when I saw how the blood was just gushing out. I grabbed the bottle of alcohol and put it on my wound. I screamed so fucking loud, I thought the whole damn building heard me. That's when I woke my sister up. The screaming must have startled her. She started banging on the bathroom door so hard that I could see the screws bulging out of the door. I opened the door, and that's when I passed out.

I woke up to her crying, saying, "Please don't leave me yet," and I was soaking wet.

She had poured massive amounts of water on my face and put tape and a gauze on my right side, where I'd been stabbed. She picked me up, helped me to lie down on the couch, and told me to get some rest and that we'd talk about it tomorrow.

No Way Out

The next morning, my sister began questioning me on what happened, how those girls looked, and where they were from. She started making phone calls, exclaiming that the shit had to be taken care of immediately. The truth was that that was my first time ever getting jumped, so I went into a shock and honestly didn't remember even if I wanted to.

Later on that week, word on the street was a couple lil niggas got hit and a bitch got shot while holding her baby at the gas station. I never asked any questions 'cause I knew that was revenge for what they had done to me.

Chapter Eleven

Jeri lost his mind. Mrs. Cee Cee worked at the Burger Café. She was, indeed, a very close friend of mine, and sort of like a mother figure. She was an older Jamaican woman and by her not being from this country, she really didn't know her way around town too well. I would help her out by showing her where different places were, especially local places that would help her to get around alone. We would go out to eat on a regular basis, and I really enjoyed her company.

Now, on this particular day, Mrs. Cee Cee had called me up, and we were planning on going apartment shopping together. I had started getting myself together. I was just about to iron my clothes and get in the shower when Jeri got in my face and started an argument. Now, that was expected of him because I had reason to believe he was cheating on me, so he needed a reason to just go ahead and do him, anyway. So, I'm sitting on the bed, ironing my clothes, and Jeri gets in my face and snatches the iron out of my hand, and then he placed the hot iron on my back and hit me with it.

I was in instant disbelief. His excuse for why he did it was that he didn't believe that I was going out with Mrs. Cee Cee. That was some straight bullshit, and he knew it. He burned me so fucking badly that I screamed so loudly that the neighbors probably heard me. My skin had melted to the core as if it was a piece of rubber. I cried just looking at the scar. I didn't know if I was coming or going. The burn was so severe that it was actually identical to the iron itself. I couldn't even sleep on it for weeks. I was so scared that I would get Jeri in trouble that I didn't even go to the hospital. It didn't completely heal until about a month later. I had third degree burns.

On Easter Sunday, I was getting dressed and totally forgot about the burn. My sister happened to be walking past as I was putting my shirt on and burst out crying. I tried to hide it, but it was too late. She said that it reminded her of *Good Times*— you know, that television show that Janet Jackson played on as a kid, where she was abused by her mom?

My sister hated Jeri so much; this really fueled her to get even with him. She was so devastated. Still, I loved him so much that I didn't want people to be angry with him even though I knew deep down inside that Jeri deserved whatever he had coming.

Chapter Twelve

Once my mind was really set on the county, working at the Burger Café wasn't going to cut it at all, and depending on Jeri's ass for help was almost like walking up to it and waiting for a response. You know that just wasn't going to happen. So, I did what I thought was best and waited for the people at an apartment complex to call me back. The lady at the rental office, Mrs. Henderson, was a real B-I-T-C-H. She kept giving me the runaround about moving in. I was calling her ass, like, every other day, and she still kept on making up excuses. She had the nerve to keep blaming shit on her boss. Finally, I got on her nerves so much that she gave me a move-in date and told me when to get my BGE cut on. I did exactly what she asked, and that day came and left, but I still didn't move in. The fucked-up part about it was that I kept taking days off at my job, saying I was moving in on those different days, and that bitch had me looking like I was lying, and she had me missing out on my money.

No Way Out

Eventually, the day finally came for me to move into my apartment. That bitch Mrs. Henderson was sitting in the rental office, cursing out one of the maintenance men named Mr. Chad, telling him how he didn't know her like that and talking about how she was from the streets.

I was sitting on the bench by the rental office thinking, *If you don't shut your old ass up trying to act young and give me my key.* After months and months of buying my household appliances, my room in my mom's house was completely packed up full of shit. I didn't have any more space in that muthafucker. I couldn't even see my room because of the clutter.

That was the day that Jeri and I were moving in together. Lord knows how scared I was, but I couldn't keep dealing with sneaking him in my mom's house, so my step dad, Leroy, Jeri, and my biological father, Flores, pitched in to help us move into our brand-new apartment.

The first night was pretty cool because we were so tired from moving all of that furniture, but the next morning was crucial. It was like as soon as we woke up, Jeri's jealous ways came. He was jealous because the apartment was in my name and he knew that any given time I could put him out, so he tried me.

I was in the kitchen cooking some breakfast. He had an attitude for no reason. All of a sudden, he grabbed the peanut butter from out of the refrigerator and threw the bottle, and it left an oily residue on the walls, and they'd painted the walls with flat paint. I called the police on Jeri and told them how he hit me and was trying to mess my house up. They came to my house and locked Jeri up.

They only charged him with destruction of property, and within twenty-four hours, he was released on his own recon. Even though I didn't want to, I had decided to be nice to Jeri because I was waiting on his share of the security deposit money that his mom had promised us. She said that she would put up two hundred dollars, and she gave it to us in the form of a check. When I took it to the rental office, they didn't accept personal checks. Once we told her that they were unable to accept checks, she switched up on me big time, and made an excuse about Jeri's name not being on the lease.

Once she saw how mad he was, she went on ahead and gave it to him and told him some shit about how it was up to him to decide what to do with the money since name wasn't on the lease. I was so fucking furious. Like, what the fuck?! The dumb bitch wouldn't allow Jeri to live with her anymore, but was telling him that it was okay to live somewhere and not be a man and pay his way.

Once she fed him that bullshit, he did exactly what I expected. That nigga didn't give me a fucking dime. He spent his money on a new cell phone and some clothes and left me struggling with all the debt that came with moving into a new place.

When they had locked Jeri up the day before, it was embarrassing as shit. They took him out of my house in hand cuffs. He was carrying on with this loud and obscene language. Mrs. Henderson was very strict at the time. You could only have the police called three times at your house. After that, they would terminate your lease. I wasn't even in my apartment a good forty-eight hours yet, and the boys had to be called. The very next day, I saw Mrs. Henderson, and she let me know that the police notified her about a domestic incident that occurred in my apartment with Jeri. From that point on, I decided that whatever happened, I would try to handle it myself or get his bitch-ass fucked up, because he definitely wasn't worth me losing my apartment over.

Chapter Thirteen

It had gotten to the point that Jeri controlled everything I did, including my money, whether I went to work or not, and if I could talk on the phone. I recall one incident where I went over to his cousin Lena's house. Me, her, and her homeboy was just chilling. Jeri stayed in our building, chilling with his homeboys that lived down the hall from us. I gave him my house key because I didn't trust him enough to give him his own key. Jeri was the type that, if given his own key, would never leave.

Lena and I were smoking hella loud, and we got real fucked up off the Goose while we were all talking and shit. Lena was trying to put me on with her home boy, saying how I didn't need to fuck with her cousin anymore and that I was too good for him. All of a sudden, Jeri called my phone, and Lena's silly ass talked Jeri up. He asked me where I was. I didn't think it was a big deal, but I never knew what to expect with Jeri.

Jeri's words were slurred, so I knew that meant trouble. He began questioning me with bass in his voice. As he was questioning me about my whereabouts, he heard a nigga's voice. He got an instant attitude and hung up on me. Lena acted as if nothing happened and just kept on drinking her beer. Her homeboy looked as if he was a little bit disturbed on the conversation he had just heard.

I left Lena's house, went upstairs to my apartment, and knocked on the door. Jeri would not answer for me. I guess he had called himself locking me out of my own house. I called Lena up and told her what was going on, and she said I could come back down and chill with them. When Jeri realized that I wasn't about to play the door game with him, he got angry, came downstairs, and started knocking on Lena's door. He was knocking so hard that Lena got scared and said that I needed to go ahead and call the police because she didn't want her neighbors calling up on her. She got mad when he continuously kept knocking at her door. He even started kicking it at four in the morning.

In a raging voice, she said, "Call the police on Jeri or you have to leave my home!"

I was trying to think of a way out, but what options did I really have? Go out in the hallway with this psycho, or wait for the police and let my rental office find out about another domestic?

To protect my apartment, I chose to go out in the hallway with Jeri and receive the ass whipping that was waiting for me. As soon as I stepped foot out in the hallway, all I could smell was liquor coming out of his pores. His eyes were bloodshot red, and all he needed was horns on his head, because I thought that I was staring right at the devil. His mug was all of the way broken down and I was so scared trying to plan an escape.

Before I could think of anything, he socked me with a right hook and dragged me down the hallway. He was trying to take me through the back stairwell and I wouldn't allow it. He picked me up off of the ground by my hair. I tried so hard to fight back, but it was like, when he was drunk, he wanted my face. I took constant blows to my head and face until I gave up, hoping that I wouldn't lose a tooth. I tried my best just to lie there and block him, hoping that he would just stop. I fell to the ground on those hard-ass stairs, trying to run from him. He caught me, and I looked down on the ground and saw a big handful of my hair just laying there.

I panicked. If he could go that far, what else could he do? As I started running again, he grabbed the back of my pants. He stretched the hell out of my Victoria's Secret night pants and started ripping my shirt off of me. I fought my way on to the elevator and made it away from Jeri. I went and got the security of the complex to call the police on Jeri. I was so embarrassed, just like all of the other times. But this time, much more badly. I was trying to cover my breasts with the little bit of shirt I had left, and when I rubbed my hair, I could feel patches falling out. I waited in the security booth for the police to come to my rescue.

Jeri and the white officer met up at the same time, and Jeri made a scene, as usual. The white officer sat in our face, eating powdered donuts with a huge smirk on his face, and that really irritated the shit out of me. Once we were arguing back and forth about our story, I could gradually see the change in the police officer, like we'd interrupted his goddamned lunch or something. I guess to him, eating donuts was far more important than me getting my ass whipped.

I tried my hardest just to plead my case, but Jeri was a natural-born actor. I mean, that motherfucker played that role in front of the officer, trying to make me look like I was crazy. I probably did look like it. I mean, my hair was all over my head, my clothes were all ripped and stretched out of place, and I was yelling, screaming, and crying. With so many mixed emotions, anxiety took over. Jeri played it so calm, like he was the fucking victim. The police made him leave, and I went back upstairs and cried myself to sleep like a newborn baby. I couldn't get much sleep that night because my body was extremely sore, and I figured that, at that time of night Jeri was sure to return since he had nowhere to go, but he didn't.

Chapter Fourteen

At this time, my grandma was in the hospital in New York City, fighting for her life. She was like a mother to me, so I was at a very vulnerable state in my life. While at the Burger Café, I ran into my home girl Tesha', who I'd known since elementary school. The good part about this was that she lived very close to my mother's house. One day, Tesh and her sister, Kellis, had invited me out with them and one of their other home girl's named Penny. I thought that it was a great idea since I had been secluded from everybody except for Jeri for so long. The girls had come up with this idea to hit up a local club around the way to meet up with this guy about some modeling shit. He wanted to meet all of us since we all were cute as fuck.

At first, I was a little hesitant since I was at my mother's house taking out my braids. Then, I was like, *Fuck that shit I could use a drink or two.* So, I lied to Jeri and told him that I was hanging out with Tesha at her house with the girls.

No Way Out

Me and the girls had gotten real fly, and you couldn't tell us nothing at all, because all of the niggas in the club was hovering all over us. My dress was expensive and luxurious and fit my body well. I put on a nice wig and some badass pumps and was ready to dance my pain away. This one nigga bought me and my homie Tesha our first drink. Just as soon as I gulped it down, someone announced my government name on the loud speaker. It was so fucking loud in there that I didn't hear it.

That's when Tesh was like, "Yo, did I just hear your last name on the loud speaker?!"

As she said it she had that look— you know, the mysterious look people do with their eyebrows when shit isn't right.

I walked over to the bouncer and asked him if someone had called me over the loud speaker, and he pointed to another gentleman. I looked down and could not believe my eyes.

I was staring right at Jeri.

The club was glass and he could see right through, but how in the fuck had he found me? I was so fucking puzzled, but I picked up the last little bit of my drink and told Tesha that I would return and just needed to handle things with Jeri right quick. I went outside to see what he was doing there, and he started flapping his lips about how I had lied to him and how he went and knocked on Tesha's door and how her boyfriend told him we came to the club to meet some guy about modeling.

I could not understand why her boyfriend/baby's father would run his mouth like a bitch. As we were talking, I was wondering why in the hell was he there. Even though he had just answered that question, it still was not enough reason for me. Before I could even get my thoughts out, Kellis popped up and asked what was going on.

Jeri replied, "I'm talking to Beauty. We're good."

Kellis pulled me toward her, wrapped her arm around me, and said, "Fuck that nigga. I want you to come with me."

In Jeri's mind, we were probably lesbian lovers and she was trying to take me away from him.

Jeri yelled, "Naw! Once we're done talking, she can go with you, but right now, I'm not finlshed with my girl yet."

Next thing I knew, Kellis started going off on Jeri, saying, "Fuck that, bitch-ass nigga!"

She set Jeri off, and he started calling her all types of bitches and had the nerve to spit on her.

Kellis went back up to the club and her crew. Meanwhile, me and Jeri were standing outside of the club, getting into it. He was hanging around as if Kellis was not on her way to get her some help. In his eyes, I was taking her side. I just wanted the nonsense to stop from both parties. My real reason for going off on Jeri was simply because he showed up. I felt like he violated my personal space and he disrespected another woman.

He got mad with the fact that I would not leave with him, and he tried to pull me in the woods beside the club. When I started getting loud, he ripped my dress, snatched my wig off, and ran off somewhere. I was humiliated once again. Hella niggas were outside hanging by the club and witnessed that shit.

Due to that loud-ass disturbance, the police arrived on the scene with twenty-one questions. I was not for that shit. I was just ready to go. I told them motherfuckers that I did not know where he went and, to be honest, I did not care. Next thing I knew, Tesha came running over to me with Kellis and Penny, talking some shit about how my boyfriend called Kellis a bitch and how he'd spit in her face and that she wanted to know why Jeri went over to Tesha's house to confront her boyfriend about my whereabouts.

The next question was, "Where the fuck is Jeri?"

Little did they know, Jeri had just jumped into a hack, and the driver sped off quick! I guess those bitches did not know me too fucking well, because Tesha and I hadn't hung out since elementary school, so that didn't really count. Since then, I was known to have a very bad temper and didn't take any shit. Of course, I was a really sweet girl as long as you didn't get me wrong.

Their other home girl started talking so loud in my face that spit was flying everywhere. She was yapping some shit about how her dude had put a gun to her face and pulled the trigger but the gun jammed. I felt sorry for shorty, I truly did, but what in the hell did that have to do with me?

They were all drunk, and we were all yelling back and forth in each other's faces. It was just me against them, but, to be honest, I felt like they weren't deep enough drunk in all. My home girl Tesh was not really saying too much of anything, which really pissed me off. I was thinking, *Why would she allow her people to get themselves caught up in my business like that?*

Me and the bitch Penny were in each other's faces so close, but she didn't buck, so I left well enough alone because, at the end of the day, the real person to blame was Jeri. He never had a right to show up, anyway. Tesha made a little joke like, "Bitch, you didn't look like that when you left the house."

I laughed a little just to stop myself from crying.

They asked me if I needed a ride home, and I declined. I called my best bitch, Kim, crying on the phone with her. Not because I was scared of anyone, but because my feelings were hurt.

No Way Out

Another fucked up night. Kim's crazy ass was asking me where those bitches were. Even though I didn't mind a good fight, at that point, I knew in my heart that the real villain was Jeri, and fighting them would not have done much for me. I brushed her off and ignored her offer. I continued talking with her as I walked home until this nice guy pulled over and offered to take me home since the club was close to where I lived.

Chapter Fifteen

Right after that club incident, we got word that my grandma was terminally ill and that she had gotten worse. We went up to New York, where she lived, to go visit her in the hospital. That time seemed so much different than the other times my grandmother had been in the hospital. My intuition was very good and, this time, when my mom mentioned her, it was like God told me she was going to leave me forever, because I just broke down and cried continuously.

We all went to the hospital to see her. She was a very petite woman, but she had lost so much weight. It was so difficult for me to see her like that. As the evening would approach, her memory would get so bad that she would forget who we were.

My sister asked my grandma if she'd eaten and how she felt.

She exclaimed that she hadn't eaten anything, and that her pain level was at one hundred percent. Mind you, this was in the day time when her memory was on point. My sister started looking at my grandmother's chart and noticed that she really had not eaten. When the nurse was questioned, she said my nana would not eat. Now, we were talking about a seventy-eight-year-old woman that was in a whole bunch of pain from cancer and could not even stand up by herself. Why didn't they at least try and feed her?

The nurses made up their lies and excuses, and shit got real ugly in there real quick. My family and the nurses got to beefing so bad that they requested that we only had two visitors in the room with her at a time.

While I was sitting in the room with her in the evening time, playing with her pretty, sliver Indian hair, she called out for me.

"Beauty!" she exclaimed, not realizing that I was already by her side.

Even though I was there, hearing her shout my name on her deathbed, it hurt me so bad too see my grandmother dying. The family and I all gathered around her to say a prayer, and, out of nowhere, she started calling on God. From that day on, I knew that she was leaving us soon and that God was calling her home.

The doctors had come back in the room shortly after that with her test results and said she only had six more months to live. That was so devastating to me; all of this had come out of nowhere.

While at the hospital, we had this rude-ass nurse who she lied and said she fed my grandma. We knew she was lying because my grandma told us. Plus, my sister worked in that field as well and they'd made a mistake and left the chart out, which said that she didn't eat that day. They had me so pissed off. When the bitch came in the room, I spit on her with no warning at all. After that, they made my family have restrictions on how many people could see my nana at one time. I hurried up and I said my goodbyes, and back to Baltimore, I went, 'cause I wasn't trying to go to jail at all.

A week after returning home, my mom and aunts went back to New York to visit my nana. After my mom and uncles left the hospital, my auntie, Janet, remained there with my grandma, waiting patiently for visiting hours to start over. Out of nowhere, my mother called me at three o'clock in the morning and got very quiet and told me she had something to tell me.

I got myself together to hear what my mother had to say.

There it was: the news I'd been dreading. My grandma had passed away. I did not know what to feel at the time. I was completely numb. I guess the worse pain I had experienced was watching her suffer so much.

As the days went on, we prepared for her funeral. She was like a second mother to me. No one knew my pain.

Jeri did one thing well. He remained by my side when I got the bad news. I had turned into a heartless and fearless person. I was very depressed. I would just break down and cry at work. I could not even handle a whole eight-hour shift.

We had to go back to New York to attend my grandmother's funeral. The day had come for me to see my nana for the very last time. She looked beautiful, and everyone had so many good things to say about her. It was hard for me to come face to face with her while she was in that casket, but I did. I walked up to her and kissed her face. There was so much tension in the family. For many years, my grandma had been the rope that tied the family together. At the funeral, they had beautiful pictures of my grandma everywhere. My nana was a stallion, even in her older days.

After the funeral, we were on our way to my grandfather's house. Him and my nana had broken up years earlier, and he had a new family. I could not stop thinking about the fact that she was gone. In front of everybody, I kind of exclaimed that I did not have any more grandparents left. That really pissed my brother off, but I really could not understand why, because I was only speaking on how I felt.

He responded to that with a negative reaction, saying something smart out of his mouth. He was showing off for his little girlfriend, but the way I felt, I was ready to throw hands on both of their asses. See, people that did not know my granddad personally would not understand how I felt. We never really got the chance to have a close relationship; we really didn't have that bond, so I felt like I really didn't know him. I would just see him from time to time.

From that day forward, things between my brother and I changed, and not for the better, because he was too busy trying to impress his bitches.

No Way Out

Chapter Sixteen

Once I got back home, I finally tried to clear my head about what had happened to my grandma. Jeri was very comforting at first. I was actually happy to see him. I was in the process of quitting the Burger Café because of all the shit going on there. Plus, those bitches kept cutting my hours, and I was on a mission. I had gone on a job interview in the photography field. It seemed fresh, new, and exciting. Even though I was a little down and out, things started looking up for me. Two days later, I got the call I had been waiting for. When I was told that I'd gotten the job, I ran around the house screaming like a mad man, and Jeri appeared to be happy for me for once.

I had been working there for a month when I got off of work and went home, where Jeri asked me if he could have thirty-five cents, and I told him no. It was not the fact that it was thirty-five cents. It was the fact that Jeri depended on me. He did not want to go out and work, and it started getting on my nerves again. The more I would say yes, the more he would ask.

He snatched my pocketbook, held me down, and then took all of my money out of my purse and ran out of the house. I called the police on his ass for taking my shit. The police came and could not find any signs of Jeri.

As soon as they left, he was back, banging on my front door like a maniac. His cousin Tammy used to live downstairs as well, so she knocked on my door pretending to want the movies she'd let us borrow back.

I asked her if Jeri was with her before I opened the door, and said told me he was not. Once I unlocked the door, he was forcing his way into my house to fight me. She was a stupid bitch for that, because he was forcing his way in while her infant child was in her arms. As soon as he got in the house, he popped me dead in my face and kept chasing me around the table like a mad man. He went in the fridge and threw some cold juice on me. His cousin Lacie, was already in the house with me, chilling. No one would help me. The sad part about it was that Lacie and I were supposed to be cool. I was trying so hard to get away from him, but he just would not stop.

After they pleaded with him about him going to jail, he finally decided to leave on his own. After that, Lacie and I had gotten real close, because she understood what I was going through with her cousin. He hated us being friends. He told me not to hang with her because she was a slut and a dummy. He had all kind of names for her, except for the child of God. I knew deep down inside that he just did not want me to have any friends. He was just that jealous and selfish. Jeri was coldhearted. If it was not about him, he did not care, even if it was his own family.

The tension was starting to build up with Jeri and I. He was being very disrespectful by staying out late. I even suspected that he was cheating with a girl that lived inside of my building that I used to go to school with. She would look at me funny as she would walk past me. It was that woman's intuition that I felt.

One day, I came home from work and Jeri was on the telephone. I got very quiet just to hear the voice, because I could tell when Jeri was being sneaky. He kept on talking as if I wasn't there. I heard a female's voice, and he kept on responding to her as if she was a male. Her voice was so familiar. It sounded just like the girl, Stacy, that I went to school with. I was very good with voices, so I knew it was her. I mean, they would play it off so good that, when I would ask questions, they would put the girl's brother on the phone.

I had really gotten so damn depressed dealing with Jeri and his bull shit that I was ready to cheat. I had met this sexy-ass light-skinned nigga named D. He had long braids,

83

pretty-ass hair, was thugged the fuck out, and could dress his ass off.

I was walking down the street on my way to my mother's house. I had just gotten off of work when he pulled over right beside me. I was digging his style, to keep it a hundred. As sexy as he was, I definitely knew that he could take my mind off of Jeri.

I told Lacie about me meeting D and how I was feeling him like that. Lacie and I had gotten real close to the point that I put her on with one of D's cousins, Lil Crazi. Me and D had gotten to the point where I would creep over to my mom's house to fuck with him for a little while to get our little quality time in. He would take me back and forth to driving school every time that I had to go. It must have been meant to be, because my best bitch used to live right across the street from D and his family for years, and D and I never met until the day that he stopped to talk to me. Kim would make jokes about D's ass and call him the little kid on the block. That was our little inside joke. She gave him that name because she remembered him when he was young, and she said he used to be bad as hell, always on that damn bike.

They were known for being big-time drug dealers with flashy cars and a whole lot of cash. If any niggas went on Roanoke Street and they didn't belong there, they were definitely in for some shit. They had a lot of niggas round there scared because they had shootouts on a regular basis. His gangster mentality really turned me on.

No Way Out

Chapter Seventeen

It was just a few days until my birthday, and I was so excited as I made birthday plans with Jeri. Then, he asked me about some pussy, and I instantly got turned off. I made up some bullshit about how I really didn't feel good. Jeri got mad and punched me so hard in my temple that I instantly saw lights, and he choked me so hard that my throat was literally burning. I begged him to stop after praying in front of him. He must have felt bad, because he stopped. I got up and went into the bathroom once he had calmed down.

I looked in the mirror, and I could not believe my face. My eye was swollen shut, and once I was able to open it, I saw a reddish ring inside of my eye. The outside of my eye sustained a purplish black color. I could not understand how a hard blow to the head could blacken my fucking eye like that. The fucked-up part about it was that I had to go to work the very next day. I tried to put some ice on it for about two hours or so, but that shit didn't budge. It was almost as if I made it worst.

No Way Out

I was disgusted. My fucking birthday was in two days. There was no way in hell my black eye would go away that quickly. I called up my job and made up a lie, saying that I had the pink eye and that the medication they gave me caused an allergic reaction. I stayed out of work and out of the company of my family and friends. The only people that knew about it were my home girls Tarsha and Kim, and those bitches were my two best friends. They knew about everything that had taken place with Jeri and me.

Out of the blue, my sister called me yelling and fussing about how nobody got to see me on my birthday, so I decided to go and meet up with her. I combed my long, pretty hair down into a rap to try and cover my eye.

My sister and I met up at the subway station. As soon as we met up, we went over to the Burger Café to get us some food and visit my bitch Tarsha. I tried so hard to cover up my eye, Lord knows I did.

Tarsha said, "Beauty, looking at your eye makes me want to cry."

Once Tarsha went to the back to get our food, my sister said, "You know that nigga is going to get fucked up, right?" She said that she could see my eye and that there was no need to hide it. She'd waited for Tarsha to leave because she didn't know if Tarsha knew about everything that was going on.

The very next day, I got up and went to work. As soon as I got there, they asked me what I was doing there since I was not scheduled until later on. Meanwhile, Jeri was calling my cell phone, talking about my brother and sister had just left the house. I did not believe him, so I told Jeri to stop lying, but he continued to go on and on about it. That's when I left the job to make my way back home, and I received a call from my sister, who told me that they knocked on my door and Jeri would not answer it. They played it off by getting on the elevator. Once they got on, they heard my front door open. My brother stayed on the elevator, and my sister poked her head out.

Jeri asked my sister if she was looking for me, and he told her that I was at work. As soon as Jeri opened up the door, my sister gave my brother the okay to get off of the elevator and go in. Once he went in, he asked Jeri why he put his fucking hands on me. Jeri lied as usual and said that he doesn't hit me. My brother told him to get up and fight like a man before he knocked his bitch ass out since he liked to fight on me. Jeri wouldn't put up his dukes to fight. He merely angered my brother, and he just straight bitch smacked him.

"Yo, we family," Jeri said. "I don't want to fight you."

My brother straight popped him again, just slapping him around like a female. After that, my brother pulled out his gun and started beating Jeri with it and told Jeri that he better not ever put his fucking hands on me again. He swore on his kids that nigga was going to die the next time. After that, my sister and brother left.

Jeri called my phone up with this fake-ass story about how my brother tried to fight him and he didn't want to fight. Not because he was not scared, but because that was my brother. Jeri knew how my family rolled, and he knew I hung around thug-ass niggas so he didn't want me to think he was a whore. I just let him keep making up his lies.

Once I got home, I noticed this big-ass hole in my bedroom wall that Jeri must have put there out of anger once they left because he got his ass whooped.

Every time Jeri and I would get into an argument after that, I would throw it up in his face how he didn't want to fight my brother, and how he only wanted to fight me because I was a girl. He would talk a little shit, but he had stopped putting his hands on me for a while because he was scared I was going to tell or that my brother might pop up. Not to mention that the day all of this stuff happened, when I went to work, everybody was staring at my eye, like they knew that somebody had just whooped my ass.

Chapter Eighteen

Jeri's behavior had gotten worse, and the tension had only grown between us. He was known to be a liar, but he couldn't fool me. Jeri had gotten this new job working at Kirby, and he had been there for about two or three weeks— just enough time to get his first pay check.

Jeri bought himself a PlayStation 2 when they first came out, a couple pairs of boots, and some clothes, and he bought me this cheap-ass necklace with a cheap-ass heart locket charm to match it. He told me that he was going to take it back, but when I called up to the jewelry store, none of these employees had seen Jeri. Still, he never came back home with the necklace.

A few days later, Jeri came in and was getting dressed up. He looked like a million bucks in the clothes that I'd paid for. I asked him where he was planning on going, since he was getting dressed up and all.

"To the bar," he replied.

"Okay, cool," I said. "I want to go."

"I want to go alone."

At that point, I knew he was lying. For one, Jeri wasn't the type to go to bars. For two, it just didn't make any sense to me, because I just knew when Jeri wasn't telling the truth. After that, a big argument occurred between Jeri and I. Once Jeri went to go downstairs in the building where we resided to go and get his underclothes out of the dryer, I went ahead and threw some sweat pants and a little tee shirt on right quick, locked the front door, and left.

I ran like a bat out of hell as fast as I could. I wanted this bastard out of my life for good. I was tired of that lying motherfucker cheating on me. So I ran, ran, and ran, and, all of a sudden, I saw Jeri. How in the hell did he find me? More importantly, how did he know which way I was going to go?

Jeri caught me. He was just too fucking fast. I was all out of breath. I was a small thing, but I definitely wasn't physically fit.

He grabbed one of my arms, and I used the other arm to call the police on him. He tried to out-slick me by calling the police on me, saying that he lived with me and all he wanted was his stuff.

By the time we got back to the house, they told me that if he stayed a night and left anything over my house, by law, he could say that he lived there. They only made him leave because of the violent things I told them Jeri had done. Jeri was pissed but clever at the same damn time. He knew that he would find some way to make his way back to my house. Besides, he wanted his freedom for the night so he could go and see the bitch he had gotten so icy for. This nigga had on brand-fucking-new everything, including boxer shorts.

No Way Out

Chapter Nineteen

Jeri beat me up again. There was blood everywhere. For a second, I thought that I'd lost some teeth. He threw me up against a car and kept banging my head on the glass. I could feel the swelling from my lip. On top of that, my left eye was swollen shut from the punches he threw. He didn't get away with it, because the police were called out, and Jeri was arrested. People were sitting inside of their cars watching and couldn't help but to call.

Jeri was wilding out on the police, and all he did was get himself into more trouble. The police took pictures of my face; I had scratches everywhere and a big bite mark on my arm. Jeri had even popped the chain belt that was on my pants, and there were tracks everywhere— another hairdo fucked up. The police were angry with Jeri, and they tried their best to comfort me, but nothing in the world could stop the pain I was feeling.

Jeri's uncle, Alex, and aunt, Tanya, bailed him out of jail. He called me as soon as he was released. We weren't supposed to have any contact whatsoever. As soon as Jeri called my phone, I answered it. I know it was stupid, but I'd invested so many years in it. I just kept that hoping that one day, he might just go back to the person he used to be. Now, we both had to try to manage sneaking around each other without having the police called because of that court shit coming up. We both could have got in some shit.

That day finally came, and we all went to court together. Me, Jeri, his mom, Trecy, his aunt Tanya, his uncle Alex and his evil-ass grandmother, the wicked bitch of the west. There were so many domestic violence cases in there. I could not believe some of the shit I was hearing in court. This one guy had beaten his bitch in the head with a house phone until she passed the fuck out. Once she passed out, he ran to get a knife, and that's when the police kicked in the door and caught him red handed.

I was nervously waiting to see what was going to happen with us. I didn't want Jeri to do any jail time. We all sat there praying for Jeri's victory, and he promised me that he would never hit me again. As sincere as he sounded, he'd made that same promise to me over a thousand times.

The couple sitting beside us went up, and the girl got on the stand and lied for her baby daddy. That's when she got caught up in her lies and the judge offered her some jail time. So,

I was petrified and didn't really know what to expect since that was my first time having to take the stand before a judge.

My heart fell right out of my body and instantly disappeared. Jeri had the audacity to be getting smart with the judge. By accident, Jeri agreed to get on the stand and ask me to be a witness. I got up on the stand and lied for Jeri, and they made me put my right hand up and swear under oath. I'm a Christian, so lying under oath was scary for me. I couldn't believe that I was actually getting on the stand to lie for Jeri, and my lies were very believable, too. The state's attorney that was prosecuting our case thought that she had me like she had that other girl, but I had her fooled. I was definitely on my A game.

The state's attorney couldn't catch me, because I didn't fold under pressure. Jeri got off easily, just like that. He won the fucking case, thanks to me. But they put it on as a stat where the case would remain open for one whole year and if Jeri did anything to violate, he would be going back to court. Jeri needed to be on his best behavior, especially to me. We all hugged each other tightly, and then we left.

No Way Out

Chapter Twenty

Everything seemed to be going pretty well for a while. I was still managing the picture spot job I was working at. I had run back into my homeboy named Richard. We'd been kicking it ever since I was a preteen, but I hadn't quite seen him since he used to take me home from the Burger Café. It was good seeing him again. He was somebody to talk to other than Jeri. It felt like magic every time that we would hook up. It was a stress reliever in a strange way because Richard knew all about my past relationships.

Richard called me up and told me that he wanted me to come over to his house. I lied and told Jeri that I was staying the night at my mother's house. Richard came to get me, and once he got there, he gave me a big old hug. We had so much to catch up on. He took me to a fancy little carry-out spot, and I got some barbeque chicken, collard greens, sweet potatoes, and some sweet honey cornbread. We went to the bar and got a pint of Henny, and then we got some good-ass loud and went back to his crib.

Richard stayed with his mom in her basement. A lot had changed for me since the last time that I saw Richard. I had my own place, a good-paying job, and a new boyfriend since the last time I saw him, but I still had a crush on him. Richard was cool as shit, plus, he always drove ever since we were, like, sixteen-years-old. He sold drugs, but he told me that he got him a little job at the nursing home. He had a daughter by this little mixed chick that he had been dealing with on and off for a few years. There was something very different about Richard that I could not put my finger on. But one thing for sure, my momma did not raise any fools, and I was going to get to the bottom of it.

While I was chilling with Richard in his room, D, my little light-skinned treat, was calling my phone. He would always come see me at my momma's house too. We were supposed to have been going to the movies that night, but I ended up hooking up with Richard, so I guessed that was why he was calling me. I could not stop smiling. D had called me twice, and I sent him straight to voicemail. I told Richard that I had to use the bathroom and went straight upstairs too call my boo.

With D, I knew that I wanted him. He was just my type. I knew that that nigga D would be the only one that could get my mind off of Jeri's ass. I lied and told D that I was at my sister's house after I found out that he had just popped up at my mother's house looking for me. I thought that it was kind of cute that D was digging me just as much as I was digging him.

I cut the conversation real short and went back downstairs into the basement with Richard, and we watched some gangster-ass movies and cuddled all night long. The first movie we watched was Scarface with Al Pacino, so you know the type of mode we were on. We did not fuck, but only Lord knows how bad I wanted to, 'cause the dick was sitting hard as shit on my ass. That was a very big turn on for me, and I got real excited as soon as he did it, but I just rolled over and went to sleep, and I got him to take me home early that morning.

Meanwhile, there was tension growing between Jeri and I. I was constantly making up excuses as to why I wasn't giving him the time of day. I had to make time for my new boos. Jeri started asking for sex again. It was sickening. I never thought that it would happen, but I was actually starting to feel like I was losing feelings for Jeri. It was getting to be weird, because the more I would push him away, the more he would pull closer to me. Jeri had really gotten clingy and even more insecure.

I got tired of lying to Jeri. I wanted to be free from him. I even felt a little bad that I had been like that to him. For some strange reason, I just could not build enough strength to leave. Out of every guy that I'd ever dealt with, Jeri would never go far. It was almost like we were soulmates. We needed each other, and I knew that after all the time we'd invested in each other, Jeri would one day get it together and give me some act right, and we would become an old, married couple with a happy ending and a whole bunch of stories to tell.

Chapter Twenty-One

After coming home from a hard day's work, I noticed that Jeri did not call me the whole entire day, which meant he was either in some type of trouble or doing something that he had no business doing. I got home to a little note on the fridge saying that his cousin had just had her baby and that he was going to the hospital to go and see them. Me being me, I was not trying to hear that shit because Jeri was afraid to take a piss without me. I had to get to the bottom of this one.

I picked up my house phone and redialed the last six phone calls back. The very last one was the time. He must have thought that I was dumb or something. With the previous ones, he had dialed star sixty-nine before the number. My heart dropped instantly, because I knew that meant he was hiding something, and I did not like it. Curiosity got the best of me, so I dialed the number, not knowing what to expect. But after dealing with his ass for almost five years, it was worth knowing what the fuck was going on. Pacing back and forth as I dialed each number

103

had me shaking. And there it was. A female answered the phone.

I politely asked the girl if anybody from that number knew anybody named Jeri. That's when she told me to hold on while she checked it out. Another female got on the phone and said that she knew a few Jeri's. Before I could even say anything else, she asked me if I was talking about the Jeri from the chat line. I said yes, knowing exactly who she was talking about. That seemed right up Jeri's alley. One of the other numbers he dialed was a chat line, so I just put two and two together

She told me that Jeri spent a lot of time talking to her on the phone. As soon as she said that, I hung the telephone right up. I'd heard all that I needed to hear. Now, I had to patiently wait in the house for Jeri to come home so that I could confront him with all of my evidence. I was really hoping that Jeri didn't call first, because I had a really hard time keeping my mouth shut, especially when I was angry.

I took a nice, hot shower and made myself a home-cooked meal. I even cleaned the whole house up. By the time Jeri got in the house, I had fell asleep on the couch. He was trying his best to figure out what I was up to, assuming, as he always did, that I didn't call him because I was out fucking around on him like he did to me when, in reality, I was only playing detective at that moment. So, Jeri came in the house and was all loud and shit. Had the nerve to fix himself a plate and didn't even wash his dirty-ass hands. Once he came in the living room, he tried to kiss me and told me how good I smelled.

I knew what that meant his ass wanted some pussy. When he kept on being in my face with that fake-ass phony shit, I just blurted it all out and said, "Fuck the bitch who you met from the chat line named Leah."

He lied and told me that his homeboy named Calvin was with him over my house one day and he was playing around on the chat line and Calvin pretended to be Jeri. I knew deep down in my heart that Jeri was lying as he always did, but at that point, I was waiting for his ass to dig his own grave, because I needed an excuse to leave his sorry ass and mess with D, anyway.

The very next day, his cousin Lacie came over and we hung out. Our intentions were to meet some niggas, some street niggas, at that. We had gotten to be very close friends, to the point where we called each other cousins. I began to confide in her about all the things that Jeri was doing to me, plus other niggas. As Lacie and I were walking to the bar, I started telling her how I thought that Jeri was cheating on me. I also told her about the conversation that me and Leah had shared over the telephone. I then asked her pregnant ass her opinion about everything that was going on between me and Jeri.

She said, "Girl, call her back so we can ask her more questions and find out what's really good."

Even though Lacie was Jeri's biological cousin, she felt like my real family, because I'd always wanted a little sister. Plus, she already knew how crazy Jeri was. At times, they would not even speak to each other because of the way Jeri always carried on.

I agreed with Lacie and decided to call the girl back and put her on speakerphone.

After we greeted each other, I told her that I was calling back about Jeri. I asked her about how long they had been talking on the chat line and, I even told her what area I lived in.

"Hold up," she said. "You talking about Jeri from Sherman Ave?"

I said, "Yeah."

"Well, that's not the one I met on the chat line. His peoples live right across the street from me, and I go to the school right around the corner from there."

Puzzled, I asked, "School? Well, if you're in school, how old are you?"

"Sixteen," she said proudly, as if that shit was cute or something.

I asked her if they'd had sex, and she said yes. All of a sudden, I felt like killing this motherfucker. I asked her if they had used protection, to which she replied, "Hell no. And I might be pregnant because I didn't come on my period this month."

"If you're pregnant how far along do you think you are?"

"About 8 weeks."

"Where did y'all fuck at?"

She began to tell me how they fucked in the park by the school and how she would give him money for cigarettes. He told her that we broke up but we lived together as roommates, and he asked her if she wanted to come over to my house and chill while I was at work. I broke it down to her very nicely, as nice as it was going to get, but I was straight up.

"You're very lucky you didn't, because if I would have caught you in my house, I would have fucked you up."

After hearing all of that, I was enraged. For one, he was sleeping with under-aged girls and, for two, he was inviting people in my house, knowing that when I came home, I checked closets, tubs, and even looked under beds and behinds sofas. It was like Jeri was really asking for trouble. A few days later, I told Lacie to walk with me up Sherman Ave, and it just so happened to be on a nice, hot summer day. Once we got to Jeri's best friend's house I saw Jeri's big head ass walking in the door.

He came over to us and was all up in my face, wondering what we were doing around there.

Once we went and sat on the porch, this little fat ass girl came out of nowhere yelling, "I'm going to tell Trisha on you, Jeri!"

I asked Jeri nicely what all of that was about. Jeri would not come out and tell me the fucking truth. That's when I got mad. He nervously said that the little girl's cousin liked him, but he did not know that I knew everything I needed to know.

I kept things going as if I didn't, and I pretended as if I was leaving from around that way. Lacie and I went around the corner to hide. I called Trisha back to see what Jeri had told her, because I already knew that the fat ass little girl was going to tell her everything. I was just waiting to see what Jeri's response was to Trisha.

Jeri told Trisha that I was his sister and that Lacie was his cousin. He even gave me a goodbye hug as they sat and watched right across the street the whole entire time. That would explain why he was rushing us to leave, talking 'bout how bad Sherman Ave was.

After being followed and harassed by all of the neighborhood niggas, we went back around Sherman Ave. We were tired of hiding from Jeri. He was the one cheating, and I was ready to put a stop to that shit. I had to question myself a thousand times. I didn't know what I was hiding for, especially since I was the bitch that stuck around through all of his bullshit. I mean, I was the one getting my ass whipped for the shit that he was out here doing to me.

I'm mad and ready to fight back. Me and Lacie went across the street, stood in front of Trisha's house, and posted up. I kept on calling Jeri's name. I was so ready to start some shit. When that didn't work, I started saying little mean and ignorant things just to provoke a fight. All that made Trisha do was call her uncle, who she said was a police officer. Truth was, Trisha wasn't really the one I had a problem with. It was her smart-ass sister. She really had a problem with her mouth. Besides, they had a whole house full of bitches in there, anyway. Technically, I was all by myself because Lacie was pregnant, so she couldn't help me. But I wasn't afraid. I was a bad bitch, and the bitched didn't want me up in their lives when I was angry.

I knocked on Trisha's door, and I could see them peeping out the window. As we started walking off, Trisha's mom came to the door asking who we were there for.

I replied, "Your bitch-ass daughters."

Trisha's sister ran outside yelling, "What's up?"

Yeah, that's that shit I liked. Without even responding, I punched her ass as hard as I could in her face.

She kept on yelling, "I can't breathe. Get her off of me, please!"

The mother started kicking me, and the other girls came outside chasing us with bottles and knives. Me and Lacie started running because I didn't want them to try and attack her while she was defenseless. Even though we ran, it didn't matter because I got to beat one of those bitches before I left.

Eventually, it had finally sunk in that the whole situation was childish and the real person I needed to be angry with was Jeri. And that's exactly what I planned to do, starting by getting even with him first. Revenge was on my mind, and it was about time I planned accordingly.

Chapter Twenty-Two

I woke up one day and I realized that I was at my breaking point. Something definitely had to give. I know I said it so many times before, but that time was different. I was at work thinking about it all day like never before. Once, I came in from work and saw one of my old coworkers from the Burger Café chilling in my house with Jeri. I didn't even want his ass there, let alone an old coworker. I mean, yo was cool and I also knew him from up Sherman Ave and all, but he did not have any place to live, and I was not having any more roommates living under my roof.

Jeri tried his best to find a reason to piss me off as I was getting my bags together to leave. I planned on hanging out with my baby, D. We had not hooked up in a while. I was going toget real icy for him once I made it to my mother's house. I mean, that boy D was icy as a bitch, so I would never let that nigga see me looking rough. Meanwhile, Jeri started walking around the house, throwing shit around and fussing about stupid stuff, so I came up with a backup

111

plan. He knew that I was not going to give him my keys. I was 'bout ready to lock his trifling ass out of my house along with his fat-ass friend Levi. It was no disrespect to Levi because he was cool with me, but his own damn grandmother put him out of her house for stealing her rent money. I was not going to have two bozos living with me for free and stealing my shit.

I put my clothes down and told Jeri that I had changed my mind and I was just a little too tired and that I was going to stay in the house. I had tricked Jeri a too many times, and he just didn't appear to be falling for it this time. Plus, I really did not know what the girl Trisha had told him or how much he knew that I knew, but I could clearly tell that he knew I was being sneaky. Out of nowhere, Jeri asked Levi to leave real quick, so I knew that meant trouble. He only wanted him to leave because he didn't want him to see what he was about to do to me.

I panicked, but I was also frustrated, not knowing if I was going to get the chance to see my nigga D or not, fucking with this asshole. That's when Jeri told Levi he would be downstairs in a second and closed the door. Next thing I knew, he'd grabbed me from behind and was choking me. Trying to hold on to the little air I had left in me, I kept trying to reach my hand in my pocket to grab a hold of my cellular phone. Once I got it, I dialed the police, and then

112

I hurriedly hung it up. I knew that my address picked up, so they would be able to tell where the emergency was. I didn't want Jeri to snatch my cell phone, but he did, and he also snatched my house phone out of the wall and popped the cords. He threw it to the ground kicked me to the floor, then he took my house keys and left. Jeri knew that in order for me to lock up my door, I had to use the keys if I wanted to leave the house, because I couldn't just turn the lock.

I ran down stairs to the security booth and waited for the police. They got there right away. By then, Jeri's ass was already long gone down the road, probably over one of his bitches' house or something. The officer told me to notify security if Jeri came back, but I had to let the police know that Jeri was very cool with the security officer that was on duty. I didn't tell the officer, but they smoked cigarettes and weed together daily. Because of their friendship, I just didn't feel safe at all. The officer had a long talk with security, and he let her know that if anything was to happen to me on her shift, she would be held responsible. He also told her that before her shift was over at six a.m., she needed to knock on my door and check on me to make sure I wasn't being held hostage by Jeri.

I was very nervous about staying in that house, knowing Jeri's capabilities, but I couldn't just leave my doors unlocked either. I just laid down, hoping and praying that if Jeri did step foot into my building, that she would notify the police immediately. After crying for several hours, I finally got me some shut eye.

At about five in the morning, Jeri came strolling into my bedroom. I started yelling and screaming because he startled me. He covered my mouth tightly and whispered that his homeboy was in the other room and for me to remain calm and that he wouldn't hurt me. I could smell the liquor on his breath. I didn't trust it, so I warned Jeri that security would be stopping by to check on me at six in the morning, which was only one hour away. That was the only thing that saved him from hurting me.

He kissed my forehead, lied down beside me, and patted me on my back. I was soon sound asleep. I tried to get myself at least a little bit of rest until security arrived, but before I knew it, there was a loud knock at the front door.

I got up out of the bed and yelled, "Who is it?"

That caused Levi to wake up because I saw him moving around on the floor.

She yelled, "It's security! Is everything okay, mama?"

Jeri jumped up out of the bed, shaking and begging for me not to open that door. I explained to Jeri that if I did not open the door, the police would have to intervene. I turned

114

around towards Jeri and whispered to him to give me my house keys back and maybe I could make things go away. He still wanted to play those childish-ass games and pretend that he didn't have them. All he did was get me even more angry by lying on top of all the other shit he'd just done. There was no way in hell he could have got into my house without using the key, so how was that possible?

I yelled to the security officer, "If he gives me my keys, then you don't have to call the police!"

Jeri insisted on playing dumb, and the security got tired of waiting because it was time for her to get off of work. I left and went downstairs with her while she called the police for me, and I waited inside of the security booth with the doors locked and watched the cameras to keep track of Jeri's whereabouts until the police arrived.

The police finally arrived on the scene, but at that point, it really did not fucking matter, because I still did not have my house keys. The police that was on the scene filled out a report, and then they escorted me to my front door, where I realized that that motherfucker Jeri had stolen my purse again. The very nice police officers issued a warrant for Jeri's arrest. Once the officers left my apartment, I gathered up a few items of mine and stumbled across a letter from Jeri, along with my house key and cell phone.

The police officers were making all kind of jokes about Jeri being a clown, and they asked a few questions about Levi. Levi had the nerve to still be laying his fat ass on my floor throughout all of the commotion, as if his ass lived there for real. One of the male officers rudely told Levi that he had to roll the fuck out. They made me laugh. It was hilarious. They escorted Levi's fat ass out of my apartment, and I packed myself an overnight bag and called my daddy to come and pick me up. The plan was for me to stay a few nights at my mom's house because Jeri had a warrant for his arrest and it was about time for him to take responsibility for his actions.

Chapter Twenty-Three

I stayed at my mom's house for a few weeks. It wasn't a bad thing, because I really enjoyed being over there, anyway. When I ran out of clothes, I called up my homie, Tarsha, to go with me. She didn't live that far from my mom's house, anyway. Once she came to pick me up, we headed straight to my apartment. I brought her along with me because I knew that I had to bring somebody that could fight. If Jeri caught me alone, he would have tried to murder me.

We pulled up to the complex and looked around. Once the coast was clear, we went up to my apartment, and I quickly packed a bag of clothes. While packing, I came up with this crazy-ass idea, like always. The idea was to go out looking for Jeri and seek some revenge.

We hopped in her truck and staked out all of the places that I personally knew Jeri to hang at. As we were on our way to look for him, the idiot called and said he was at Mr. Tony's house and he was using his cell phone to call me. I think the point of him telling me that was because Mr.

117

Tony didn't live that far from me. I hung up, called the police, and gave them Mr. Tony's cell phone number, hoping that they would trace it back to the address where Jeri was located so that he could be arrested on sight. My plan did not work, and Jeri was still running around scot-free, thinking he was untouchable, which only angered me more. At that point, I didn't know how much more I could take.

Tarsha came up with the idea to go up Sherman Ave, his stomping ground. We parked directly across the street from his grandmother's home and two doors down from his best friend's house. I put my fitted cap on and leaned back in the chair with my black Fendi shades on to disguise myself. Low and behold, who did we see? No one but Jeri's ass! He was walking through the alley without a care in the world. Too bad his stupid ass did not see what was coming to him. He looked directly at me, but he was so busy trying to be a player, I wasn't quite sure if he noticed us or not. I nervously asked Tarsha if she thought Jeri recognized us.

With lots of confidence, she smiled and said, "Naw, we're good, shorty."

He turned back around and glanced at the truck. Tarsha yelled and told me to duck down. As I was ducking down, I proceeded to call the police again. Once the 911 operator answered the phone, I began to inform her that Jeri had a warrant for his arrest and how we knew his current location. She told me to just be patient and that they would be sending an officer out promptly.

This seemed very unreal to me. It felt more like I was in a movie and, in any moment, I could make this disappear. I didn't really know if I was doing the right thing. At that point, I was tired of protecting Jeri when he acted as if he didn't care what happened to me or him. All Jeri had to offer me was his ass to kiss. I decided that it was time for him to pay for his actions, and that was all I knew.

We remained ducked down in the truck for what felt like a very long time. I lifted my head up a little just to see if Jeri was still in sight. I took a glance at my watch and saw that it had been over twenty minutes since I'd called the police. I sat in an instant daze, just wondering where in the hell could the police be. We decided to call back. I notified the operator that we called a few times previously and no one came out to assist us. That's when she let me know that the shift changed and it would probably be a while before an officer would be arriving.

I had finally developed the strength I needed to be completely done with Jeri, and no one was around to save me. How fucking convenient. Jeri had gotten away again because they never showed up, so we had no choice at all but to leave.

No Way Out

Tarsha took me back to my mother's house because I really needed to relax. That shit was really getting the best of me. I was completely frustrated. Jeri had started calling me every single day, back to back. He would call making up all of these lies and begging me not to press charges against him. Deep down inside, I really did not want to, but I needed to have Jeri out of my life for good, and he just would not leave me alone on his own. I had no ideas where Jeri had been staying, but I was very curious. With my detective work, I was pretty confident that I would find out promptly. But before my investigation could start, the little chick hit my phone and confirmed her pregnancy and stated that she was planning on keeping the baby.

That following Monday, I got off of the bus, coming from work at about five o'clock that evening. I felt comfortable since it had been quite a while since my last run in with Jeri. I got off the bus at my designated stop with no hesitation at all, and I looked up to see Jeri standing right in front of my building smoking a cig. My eyes got big, and I began yelling and screaming as I ran down the street away from him because he was chasing me and he could run really fast.

There were people still getting on the bus. I was yelling, "Wait!" I hoped that just one person would hear me because the bus was ready to pull off, and I knew that I could not outrun Jeri. I was running like a bat out of hell while yelling for somebody to stop the bus, and it worked. At that very moment, I felt like the Lord had spared me. The bus driver stopped the bus and, just as Jeri tried to grab the back of my shirt, the driver closed the door and pulled right off. Out of breath and all, I managed to smile at Jeri sarcastically. As I was walking toward the back of the bus, Jeri threw his hands up and blew me a kiss.

I found me a sit by the window and went into a deep daze as tears flowed down my eyes. I had become a stranger to my own home, and all I could do was return to my mother's house.

I called up my bitch Tarsha and put her down with what just happened with Jeri and me. I mean, I couldn't really talk to nobody else about it, because they would never understand. She got real upset and said that something needed to be done about Jeri's ass, and I agreed. We decided to go back to my house and gather up all of his things and put his clothes and shit in the nearest dumpster. Most of his clothes were shit that I paid for, anyway, so he wasn't going to be seeing other bitches in style, at least not on my account.

I quickly gathered up all of his belongings, except for all of the things I wanted to keep. We then hopped right in the truck and headed for Tarsha's house to put his shit in the dumpster around her way, where he could never find it.

No Way Out

Once we got there, I felt a little bad about it. But when I thought about the fact this nigga was having a baby on me, the guilt went away.

We dumped everything that we bagged up, and I actually found a sense of relief when we were done. I could not believe this nigga was having a baby on me. It hurt me even more because I had aborted my baby because of Jeri's behavior and, after all of those years, someone else was carrying his child.

Chapter Twenty-Four

I waited about a month before going back to my apartment. I really need to check on it. Plus, I had been stretching my clothes as long as I could. It was definitely time to go back and get some more clothes. I was staying at my mom's house until our new court date, trying to avoid conflict. I called my daddy to take me past my house. I liked when my father would come with me, because Jeri was too scared to try anything with him.

Me and my father walked in the house at the same time. Once we got in there, I noticed that my house smelled like freshly cooked bacon and eggs, which was strange since I hadn't been there in over a month. There was no reason in hell that I should have been smelling food. I was puzzled, but I did not mention it to my father. I just went looking around the house like everything was normal. I walked into my bedroom, went over to my closet, and started grabbing some clothes to take with me. That's when a hand reached out and grabbed me.

No Way Out

Jeri jumped out and put his hand over my mouth to muffle my scream. As he held his hand over my mouth, he whispered for me not to say a word. I could not keep quiet any longer; I went the fuck off up in there instantly. When Jeri stole my key that last time and wouldn't give it back, it was because he needed to make a copy first. His objective was to scare me from my own house so he could have a place to live. He had been living there for a while without my knowledge, and he had the nerve to be cooking my goddamn food that I paid for.

That's when my father heard my outburst and burst in my room with his gun. He pulled it out and aimed it at Jeri. He was ready to cock it.

I yelled for my father to stop. I didn't want my father going to jail over that knucklehead. My dad kept one eye closed and the other one was wide open. I ran behind him and grabbed the gun while trying to get him to see that Jeri was not worth it.

I called the police and told them that Jeri had snuck into my home without my permission. I tried to diffuse the situation, but my dad didn't play about his baby. At that point, he was over it. He had already warned Jeri plenty of times before of what the repercussions would be if he put his hands on me again. My daddy told Jeri that he had already raised me and that he ain't even whoop my ass, so he damn sure was not going to allow a nigga to think he could.

While waiting on the arrival of the police, I began to think about the time Jeri and I were leaving my mother's house to walk to the subway station. We were at a light and a funeral procession was passing, and the limo driver was staring at me as they were passing by.

Jeri yelled, "What the fuck is your bitch ass looking at?"

About ten big-ass niggas jumped out of the car, ready to beat Jeri's ass. He was terrified. He tried to lie, and that's when one big-ass nigga grabbed him. I played it off and said he was yelling at me. Jeri was begging and pleading for his life. He told the sumo wrestling-looking guys that he would never disrespect a funeral. One of the niggas knocked Jeri's ass out cold and jumped back inside of the funeral car with the tinted windows. For the life of me, I could not understand why it was so easy for him to fight me.

I snapped back into the present time after I heard the knock from the police at the front door. That's when Jeri was arrested for breaking and entering.

No Way Out

Chapter Twenty- Five

After sitting in jail for about four months, Jeri finally received his court date, which my father attended with me. It was us against his mom, grandma, aunt, and uncle. While sitting in court, right in the middle of the case, Jeri and his family had the audacity to lie and say that Jeri still lived with me.

I told the state's attorney that if they needed some proof in my defense, I could prove it by asking my landlord, Mrs. Henderson, and use her as a witness, if need be.

Jeri started asking about his belongings, which he'd left at my house. I couldn't lie— I was a bit nervous, because I knew I threw all of his clothing away, and after he destroyed all of my shit, there was no way in hell that I was giving him back any of his valuables.

Meanwhile, his family kept shaking their heads and rolling their eyes at me and my father. His grandma's evil ass had the nerve to say 'God bless you' to me.

Jeri ended up getting probation, and they put our case on another stat, which meant that if he did anything else wrong within one year, I could just reopen the case. And I didn't have to pay him anything. But I still kept my restraining order out on Jeri.

After court, my father dropped me off home. I was a bit drained. I was still upset with the fact that Jeri acted as if he didn't even notice me, but I just went home and listened to some Beyoncé. It was official; we had finally broken up. It was time for me to find a way to get over that nigga. With him gone, I could finally get my peace back, have money in my pocket, and stop worrying about getting my ass whipped all day long. It was going to be hard, but Stella had to get her groove back, and I was prepared to do whatever it took.

Chapter Twenty-Six

I finally started getting really close to Richard. I was going over to his house, like, every other night. He always gave me money, and he had a career at the nursing home. He kept a car, which was a plus, and I knew his whole immediate family. After just a few months of us dating, we seemed to be getting pretty close very quickly.

His mother's boyfriend lived there, as well as his brother, Marvin. Richard's father died when Richard was a very young boy, and he'd left Richard's mother a million dollars. She had bought herself a big-ass house right out in the county. They had been living there ever since I had known them. Richard had been wanting to step up to the plate and be the man that I had been longing for, but I had to be completely done with Jeri first.

Once I finally cut all ties with Jeri, Richard asked me if he could have that number one spot in my life. You know I couldn't turn that one down. The only real problem that I had with him was that he had a child, and I'd always had a complex about niggas still fucking with their baby's mothers. Not to mention that Richard had already told me a story about him fucking his baby's mother's sister before. There was really something different about Richard. I just could not put my finger on it. Every time I was around him, he would just seem so extra relaxed. I really didn't think too much of it because he told me how he had fucked a nigga up so bad that he dislocated his shoulder. They eventually had to put a steel plate inside of his shoulder, so the doctor had to prescribe him narcotics such as Oxycodone and Percocet to relieve his pain.

His mother's boyfriend was a married man, and his wife knew all about Richard's mom. His name was Chris. Richard's mother, Nancy, had gotten into a terrible accident and, once Chris found out, he had a severe stroke. From that moment on, he wasn't the same. Chris's wife had decided that taking care of her ill husband was too much to deal with, so she paid Mrs. Nancy off to deal with him and move him in with her. He and Nancy had been dealing with each other for about twelve years, but he had been married for over twenty. I could never understand how a woman could give her husband to his mistress and not have a problem with it.

Mrs. Nancy really seemed to have taken a liking to me. I would do nice things for her like help her clean, vacuum, and wash her dishes even though I wasn't big on eating from people's houses. When Mrs. Nancy would cook dinner, and offer me some, I didn't want to hurt anybody's feelings, so I got into the habit of telling them that I had just ate, or that I would try some later. I tried my best to eat dinner before I would get over there. I couldn't lie— sometimes when Mrs. Nancy would cook, that food would smell good as a motherfucker. Not being funny, but their house wasn't the cleanest house to be eating from and they damn sure wasn't the cleanest of people.

Richard stayed in his mama's basement and kept two big ol' pit bulls. He eventually let the dogs mate so that he could sell the puppies. Once they started the mating process, they had puppies, and he kept all of those stinking-ass dogs on the other side of his basement. There was blood, piss, and dog shit everywhere, not to mention the dogs' natural stinky smell. To top it off, his mother had patients living in their home with them for extra money.

One of their main patients was Mr. Chris. Since he had a stroke, he would piss on the bed that he that Mrs. Nancy shared. From time to time, once Mr. Chris would go back to his right state of mind, he would try to run away. Last but not least was another sick lady. She was seventy-two years old. She wore Pampers, and she needed to be fed, bathed, and watched daily. Mrs. Nancy was the lady's sole care provider. I didn't really feel as though their house was that sanitary enough to eat from.

After a while, the same old line I was using had gotten played out. One day, after I spent the night at Richard's house, he asked me what I wanted to eat, and I told him Southern Blues. I couldn't deny my hunger because I'd been over there for too long without eating that time.

He instantly threw a temper tantrum and yelled, "You haven't been eating any food since you been over my house. What the fuck? You don't like to eat?"

I brushed it off, and then we laughed about it, but I made his ass take me out to get some food.

Once we were back in the house with our food, we started eating, and he started telling me that he talked to his ex-girlfriend and how she really wanted to buy one of his puppies. I caught an attitude instantly. I had heard so much about that girl. The bad thing about it was that, about a year before Richard and I started dating, I had run back into him. I had a habit of calling him out of the blue. We did this on and off for several years. I had called his phone, and he answered, then he hung up. And by me calling from my job phone, she kept on calling back and hanging up, playing on the damn phone, but this was during my Burger Café days. Tarsha just so happened to be at work with me and put that hoe dead in her place. So, with all of that bullshit that happened, I wasn't going for none of that shit about his ex, Kema, just being cool, and he was saying how much she loved dogs and he was thinking about giving her one of them.

No Way Out

Chapter Twenty-Seven

Back in the day, I used to mess with Richard's homeboy. That was a very long time ago. His name was Antwan, and he was kind of funny looking. He kind of looked like a beetle, and Richard and a few of the other homies had told me some weird stories about how some girl that Antwan slept with had given him crabs and how he was scratching for days. That was enough to scare me off. Of course, we never fucked because I wasn't digging him like that. We would talk on the phone from time to time. I never really saw too much of him because his mom was mean as shit, so we never really spent any time together. I wouldn't really call it dating, but in the eye of the public, it looked very bad. As far as me and Richard, we didn't know how to come out and tell people about our relationship. It seemed a little superficial. Things were moving just a little too fast for me, but I was going with the flow.

Ever since the accident occurred with Mrs. Nancy, she had to walk with a cane and was on some type of medication. Being around her

135

enough, I realized that she had a very bad gambling habit, which was out of this world. Every single week, that lady would go out of town to gamble and play the lotto. It was to the point where she would go to the local mini casinos in the city that I knew absolutely nothing about. It was evident that she had a problem and needed some type of help, because normal people would not spend their in a casino.

There were lots of changes going on at my job at that time; me being a store manager now required too much work. I had to work every single weekend and, since my boss did not trust anybody other than me, I would be the only person there running things. It was all because the previous store manager had stolen over ten thousand dollars from them. She would put the money in the safe and, when nobody was around, she would take all of the deposits out of the safe and spend half of the money on her crack head boyfriend, who just happened to be a black dude. I guess you could say he was juicing the shit out of that white girl. She was so damn dumb that she almost got federal time behind that bullshit and had even tried to set me up when I was the assistant manager.

She would give me the safe combination, knowing that, at the time, I wasn't supposed to have it. I had no idea this cruddy bitch was taking my drops. Luckily, the lady that worked right next to us spoke up. Mrs. Tia was her name. She had become an official witness, saying that when the money truck would come, she would tell Willie Mae to get the money together for their pick up, and Willie Mae would insist there was none. How was that so when we were open seven days a week? She had several people stating that she would buy all of her employees' lunch at all kinds of fancy restaurants at the inner harbor.

Willie Mae would call out on the regular, and that began to wear and tear on me. Her boyfriend was a middle-age black man that was on drugs. She would buy him all kinds of expensive clothes. At the time, I couldn't understand how she could afford all of these fancy items since she only made a little bit more money than I did. I can't forget the fact that she had four kids to take care of.

One day, I had gone into work, and Willie Mae said that I couldn't tell our boss, but she wanted to give me the combination to the safe for emergency purposes only. I really didn't think too much about it. I thought she was just planning on calling out or something, so if I had access to the safe, I would not have to bother her on her days off. For about a month and a half, she kept on calling out or leaving work early, making up all kinds of excuses. She would rotate our schedule and on the days I was supposed to get off of work early, she would call out. One Saturday, she called to the job, making up a lie about her kids being sick and how she had nobody else to take of them. This time she was one lie too short, and I was fed the fuck up.

I hung up with Willie, called our district manager Jenny, and put my two weeks' notice in. The very next day, I called up to the job, and Willie Mae answered the phone. I told her that I wouldn't be working there anymore and that I knew she was stealing and that I didn't trust her, and that some sneaky stuff was going on around there. She asked about the sneaky stuff, and I just hung up on her.

I was very frustrated and all of this was just built up in me. Not long after, I found a security job working for some Africans. Once it was time for me to collect my check, they kept making excuses. I did not understand why, and I became furious because I had to pay my rent. I would call up there every day, and it was excuse after excuse after excuse. I finally decided to pop up and go see if Mrs. Jenny was there, and she was. She took me in the back of the store in a private room, coming at me with all sorts of questions. That's when I found out that Willie Mae quit right after I did. Mrs. Jenny asked me some questions about our cash drops and told me that some of me and Willie's deposits were missing— ten thousand dollars' worth, to be exact.

My eyes got big in disbelief. I didn't know what the fuck was going on. I was sitting there wondering if the police were in the other room. All I knew was that I didn't have any knowledge of that bullshit, and that's when it hit me. The bitch gave me the safe combination in an attempt to set me up.

Jenny told me to write a statement of all that I knew and said that she believed me. Jenny also told me that Willie had told her a totally different story from what actually happened. She wished that I would have come forward about all the stuff that was going on a long time ago. She did not want me to leave, and she told me that the company was suing Willie for theft, and that they had taken out federal charges against her, so she was facing some federal time. The feds had already issued a warrant for her arrest, and their plans were to prosecute to the fullest extent of the law.

Mrs. Jenny gave me my check, and then we said our goodbyes. Jenny and I parted on good terms.

I started working at the security company for about two weeks. They had me working at different sites. One place they had me working at was a store out in bumba fuck with no air conditioning when it was over one hundred degrees outside. That was my last day, and I called my dad to come pick me up from there early. It felt hotter in their store than it did outside. I called Mrs. Jenny and asked her if I

No Way Out
could come back. She welcomed me back with
open arms.

Chapter Twenty-Eight

Richard loved the fact that I was a manager; it really excited him. He would go around telling everybody that I was a boss bitch. He loved the thrill of me hiring, firing, and telling people what to do. He would watch me when I was doing the schedules for my employees at his house. Sometimes he would just look at me and smile. I had gone to work one day with the strangest feeling. I did not know what it was but something was not right. The company had gotten so many complaints about our photography stand that it was ridiculous. The owner of the building had threatened to put us out so many times. We had many photography stands all over the world, but our store seemed to have the most problems. I can't lie— Mrs. Jenny really did fight for us. One of the building employees walked past and said "sorry to hear that u all are leaving us". I was surprised because that day Mrs. Jenny was supposed to be having an employee meeting with all of us. She never did tell me why, which was short of puzzling since I was the store manager. The whole day had seemed like it was

141

going wrong. After two p.m., our checks still hadn't come in, and Mrs. Jenny was running late for our meeting. I finally called her and told her that a gang of our employees had come up to the job looking for their checks she than admitted she had them and should bring them once she got there. She just wanted to make sure that everybody made it to the meeting.

Jenny finally arrived at the job. She said that she was sorry to inform us that we were closing down. Due to some of the previous issues that went down, they had decided they no longer wanted us to rent that space in their building. We all got so quiet you could hear a pen drop. We might have all had our differences, but we had become like family. We all had tried our hardest to hold back our tears. The craziest part about it was that I had just hired this guy and he said in front of all of us that he was offered another job around the same time but he decided to come and work for us. He had so many personal issues going on at home he didn't know what to do. Jenny told me that I would get a few checks of severance pay and that I would still receive my unemployment. But she did state that the company was going to try to fight the other from getting their unemployment. We all hugged each other tightly, and then we departed. I had tears in my eyes. I was so lost. I couldn't lie; it was tiring working there, but Lord knows that I needed my job. I went home and cried. I didn't know what I was going to tell Richards incentives he looked up to me so much. What he was going to think about me now that I no longer the boss, but unemployed? I started thinking about all of the events leading up to this. Like, the girl named Sarah was supposed to go inside of the dolphin show and take pictures while the trainers were getting the dolphins to do some tricks. This dummy waited until after the dolphin show was over, picked up the stick that the trainers use for the dolphins, and plunged it in a Dolphins mouth. That made the dolphins very aggressive. They tried to pull her in the water with them. The customers began to take pictures of Sarah fighting with the dolphins, which made the managers of the building angry. Jenny made Sarah write a letter apologizing for what she had done so that they would not fire her. Not long after that, we had to close down just like that, everybody was out of their jobs.

No Way Out

Chapter Twenty-Nine

Being that I was laid off and had so much free time on my hands, I lied and told Richard that I was on vacation. For some reason, he did not believe me, and he would make little jokes, asking me if I'd gotten fired. Deep down inside I was hurt because he looked up to me very much. I almost felt like I had let him down.

I stayed at his house for about a week straight, and we started arguing nonstop. That motherfucker had the nerve to call up to the job to see if someone would answer. The operator came on saying that the number was no longer in service. He put the phone up to my ear so that I could hear what the operator was saying, and then he said he knew that I had gotten fired and started laughing. He really started changing. He had become so mean.

The whole time I was over, I noticed that he had not been to work either. As I was about to ask him to take me home, there was a loud knock at the door. I didn't get to see their faces because Richard told me to remain in the basement. He said that it was the Columbians.

He went upstairs and I heard them talking to his mom. I called myself being slick and trying to turn the television down. I heard them asking for their money, but Mrs. Nancy and Richard didn't have it. They started getting really loud.

I started putting on my pants and my shoes, and I then turned the volume down on my cell. Those men had accents. It sounded like it was at least four of them inside of the house.

Richard began yelling, "Not my mom. Please, take me!"

I really was scared, but the dogs were in the basement. I knew that if I ran out to the patio, the dogs might have started barking or maybe even bit me. Richard had the back part of the basement sealed off because he knew I was afraid of them, so if I was there he wouldn't let them run loose unless he was trying to be funny.

I heard gunshots, then I heard another gun.

Mrs. Nancy kept on screaming and, with that accented voice, somebody yelled, "Shut up, bitch!"

I'm pretty sure they had no idea that I was in the basement, and I didn't want them to find out. By me being so little, I hid behind the sofa, and that's when I heard them running out of the front door, along with the sound of gunshots. I thought the coast was clear, and that's when one of those men yelled, "Check the whole house, and clean up this mess."

One guy came downstairs. I was so nervous. He didn't do much checking for witnesses. I could hear him standing on the step. Once he looked and there was no one in sight, he ran back upstairs and said that the coast was clear. I guess the boss man was upstairs checking out the scene.

I heard the front door slam. I gave it a few minutes, and then I ran upstairs to see if anybody was hurt. I saw Mrs. Nancy laying on the floor with blood gushing from her head. It looked as if someone hit her in the head with a gun. She had also been shot, and Richard was nowhere to be found. I picked up their house phone with a shirt, called the police, and told them there was a woman in there dying.

I grabbed my little bag and left through the back door. I had to go. I had ran and ran, crying at the same time. I didn't know where to go, or what in the hell had just happened, for that matter. I kept running, watching myself surroundings carefully. For all I know, Richard might have been trying to kill me because I knew too much. As I was running, I ran across this old white guy at an apartment building a few blocks from where Richard lived. He was sitting on the steps reading a newspaper.

I asked him if I could use his cell phone. He let me use it, and I called Leroy and asked if he and my mom could pick me up and they said that they would come tomorrow. They did not know how serious this was, and I couldn't tell them. With tears in my eyes, I hung up, and that's when the old man said he would take me. I was so cautious of everything that I didn't want to use my phone in that area.

The very next day, Richard text my phone, letting me know that his mom was in the hospital with a minor concussion and that she had taken a gunshot to her chest. Thanks to me, they were able to perform surgery in time stop the bleeding. The police put her in protective custody because they believed that if those people found out that she was still alive, they would surely be back to finish what they'd started.

Richard said that one of his homeboys was killed by those guys, and that they'd dipped his friend's whole body in acid. I was terrified. He told me not to worry. He wasn't going to protective custody. He planned on running and going after them for what they did to his mom. I thought that Richard had lost his goddamn mind. Who was he fooling, thinking that he could run up against some niggas like that? I was so speechless that I did not respond! At that point, I didn't know what to think. I didn't trust him anymore. I had no idea him and his mother were working with big-time drug dealers. To be perfectly honest, in my mind, distance was the best thing because I needed some clarity on everything.

The next day, I was laid up in the house bored as shit, just thinking about all that happened. I was a little paranoid, wondering if Richard was going to somehow involve me in all this bullshit if came down to it. This nigga knew my government name. While thinking about Richard and all that was going on, my mixed emotions got the best of me. I reached over to the dresser and picked up my phone. I had decided to give him a ring.

There was no answer, so I quickly hung up. That's when my phone started ringing. It was him calling me back, whispering from an unknown number. I was thinking that something was seriously wrong with that motherfucker. I asked him why in the fuck he was whispering, and he said he had his daughter with him at a hotel and he had just put her to sleep. I was wondering why he would take his daughter on the run.

Before I could say anything, he said he'd gotten her because he knew it would be a while before he got to see her again with everything that was going on.

He said, "Baby, I miss you so much. I'm about to take a little nap with her. Once I wake up, I will call you."

Disappointed, I frowned. "Okay."

Before we hung up, he said, "Don't call me. I will call you."

149

I did kind of miss him, even though I knew I could not be around him for a while, at least for my safety. A few minutes later, my cellie rang again. It was from Richard's, I smiled, thinking, *This man just can't resist me.*

"Hello, baby."

I heard another voice— one that belonged to a female. I couldn't believe my ears, so I said hello to the young lady.

She promptly asked, "Did you call this number for Richard earlier?"

"Yes. Who's this? His cousin?"

"Naw, this is his ex-girlfriend Kema, and I've been chilling over here for a few days. Richard told me that he was trying to work things out, especially because I might be pregnant with his baby. He even let me bring all of my clothes over to their other house and wash them, not to mention how much Mrs. Nancy loves me. I even went to see her at the hospital."

I was puzzled. "Damn, really? I surely couldn't tell since they talk about you like a dog. For starters, Mrs. Nancy bitch ass would talk about how they would let you hold the car to sell your pussy and how could her son wife'd a hoe."

That's when Kema began to tell me how Mrs. Nancy told her that she believed that I was anorexic, and how I didn't like to eat, and they thought I had an eating disorder. I had to explain to her that the reason I did not eat at their house was because their house was so fucking nasty.

They were definitely playing sides, telling both of us how they wanted us to live in their house. Kema was very shocked and angry once she realized that she wasn't the only one being told this, she began snitching about everything. She told me that Richard was strung out on drugs. This consisted of Xanax, Perc, Oxy, weed, and Lord knows what else. She claimed that Richard was so strung out that he climbed into his mother's window just to steal her drugs. She also said that he started using drugs when the doctor prescribed him the drugs from hurting his shoulder.

The more I dealt with Richard, the more I had come to realize how much I really did not know him at all. To top it off, Kema admitted that he had had her trying drugs, too. He had gotten her so fucking high that she urinated all over herself while her in Richard was in the bed. That would explain why, when we had gone out one time, Richard and I were sitting at the drive-thru window waiting for my food, and he was nodding the fuck off, claiming to be tired. Another time, his mother fell asleep with her head in the birthday cake. There were just too many coincidences. Everything was coming back to me at once. How could I be so blind? I really had to question myself. Richard even fell asleep on the toilet before when I stayed a night at his house. And his brother Marvin, you could look at him and tell he was doing some really hard

151

drugs. We really didn't hear too much from him because he was in and out of jail.

Kema also told me how Richard would give her money whenever she wanted and how he sat around and collected disability. I was shocked at how he lied about everything, because he'd told me that he was working at a nursing home, and I decided to do some research of my own and call. None of the nursing home employees knew anybody by the name of Richard. All I could do was stare at the phone in shock.

I had become very drawn to Keema. Richard had bragged about her so much, how she was about her money, and how she was a fly ass bitch. Just from talking to her on the phone, I could tell that shorty was a real-ass bitch, because I only vibed with the realest. We had both decided that we were going to leave Richard alone. It was for both of our best interests. I wasn't going to allow him to bring me down.

Chapter Thirty

It had been a few weeks since I'd seen Richard. Oh, boy, did I miss him. I guess when you're so used to being in relationships, it starts to get lonely when you're single. I didn't think it was truly him that I missed, but I surely did miss laying up with someone.

Richard called me out of the blue and told me how sorry he was for all of the hurt that he had caused me. It did really good to hear his apology. It was so good that I had decided to take him up on his offer when he asked me to come over and visit him. So, he came over to pick me up and we had make-up sex, but things didn't feel the same anymore. I felt bad that I even wasted my time fucking him. It was so disgusting that I felt like I had fucked a crackhead or something. Most importantly, I felt like I had let Keema down, because we'd made an agreement that we both would cut him off. The relationship was dead, and there was no reconciling. I no longer believed anything he said out of his mouth.

153

Plus, he just seemed like a bum-ass nigga to me now.

While I was lying downstairs watching TV by myself, he was upstairs, fussing with his mother about something. I didn't even bother to listen. I just stayed isolated in the basement with his dirty-ass dogs. While watching my favorite show, I caught myself dozing off, but I couldn't get comfortable in that house without knowing when those drug dealers would be returning.

That's when Richard ran down the stairs a little upset. He started throwing shit and yelling, "Why would I try to fuck that old-ass lady?"

I was so confused. Every time I came around this idiot, there was some bull shit. I sat quietly, giving him the cue to finish the story. He said that the seventy-two-year-old woman that was living there made claims to her family that she did not feel safe around him anymore because he had supposedly touched her breasts and fondled her private areas. He swore up and down that he would never do no sick shit like that, and then he turned around and asked me what I thought. I tried my best to go around the question because I didn't want to tell him how sick I thought that he and his family were.

I was dropped off to my house. I called up Keema and let her know that I spent the entire weekend with Richard and how awful it was.

She giggled sarcastically and said, "You're still fucking with that clown, I see."

154

I laughed as well. I told her about the conversation that Mrs. Nancy and Richard had had about him trying to fuck that old-ass lady. That's when she told me that his mom was a big-time drug dealer.

I was shocked. I thought Mrs. Nancy was a nice old lady, but it appeared that they all had skeletons in their closets, because I was all wrong. Those people were scam artist. They told us the same old story about how they wanted us to get married to Richard and get the extra car fixed up, and that they wanted us to move into her house and add our names to the house so that if something happened to Mrs. Nancy, we'd always have a place to live. Keema was livid when I told her about Richard and the old lady but we laughed that off too.

I was glad I decided to take all my belongings home with me, because I had decided I was never going back to seeing Richard again, but he was going to have to find out the hard way.

No Way Out

Chapter Thirty-One

Meanwhile, I started hooking up with D's fine ass all the time. I really wanted him, but deep down in my heart, I knew that he wasn't the settling down type. He was a straight up-ass nigga, and I was not used to that, but I liked it. He made it clear from the start that he did not want a relationship, but that did not stop me from seeing him regularly. I needed something fresh and new to take my mind off Jeri, because Richard really wasn't a factor. It was funny too me. I was really missing something, though I could not quite grasp what it was. I was so use to being in a relationship it felt very awkward being alone.

That nigga D was also known as Danger. He was young, crazy, cool, and real. I was trying figure out how I lucked up and got the nigga of my dreams. I told all my bitches about him, because he was something to brag about. Plus, that nigga was getting that money. I thought I might have hit the jackpot with him.

He came to pick me from my mom's house one day, and we stopped at the gas station. This nigga came back with, like, eleven cigarillos and was blasting Boosie's *You Don't Know My Struggle* in the whip, plus, he had a whole bunch of money in his pocket.

I can't lie, I was feeling him. I was ready to take them drawers off 'cause this nigga had me faded, and he knew he did because of the smile I would give him every time I saw him.

Every time Danger would come around; I would look like a million bucks. He never got to see my bad days. I would always look like I stepped out of a magazine, even if we were only going to the store. I could tell that he was really digging me too, even though he had other bitches. I knew the exact moment when I had become his main girl, and I was happy with being just that.

One day, I let him come over to my house. We were sitting on my sofa, and in the middle of a conversation, he pulled out his dick. Man, that nigga was packing. I would have liked to pass the fuck out. My eyes had gotten extremely big. I was shocked that his little skinny ass was packing like that. I told him I was almost scared for my life, and we laughed about it and he kept on rolling up that blunt. He had some piff. I was grinning from ear to ear, looking at him as he licked the blunt. He gave me crazy eye contact that made me blush. I was now ready to get high and fucked at the same damn time. He rolled up three blunts and passed them back and forth amongst the two of us. I was high as shit and he just kept staring at me. The more he looked, the more I smiled. I had not been that happy in a long time. Even though I was thinking to myself, *He's going to break my lil ass in half.*

Danger put the blunt down and began blowing inside of my ear. Lord knows I had no idea what the hell he was doing, but it felt good, so I wasn't going to stop him. He was a very aggressive young thing, pulling on my hair, kissing on my back, and licking on my belly button.

My legs clasped his neck. He sucked my sweet juices, and then he gently pushed his love inside of me. I pulled his pretty hair as I sucked on his neck. He was all a girl could ever ask for.

He threw me on the bed and slapped my ass, then forcefully thrusted his love inside again. As he was checking out my ass, he grabbed my titties and started sucking on my boobs from the side while fucking me from the back. It felt so good, I didn't want him to stop.

He slipped up and told me that he loved me for the first time. After we finished, he pulled me close and kissed my forehead, and then we both got into the shower to clean off. It lasted for a good thirty-five minutes and, afterwards, we laid down and cuddled, watching movies until we fell asleep in each other's arms.

D started spending a lot of time with me, but he would have his moments where he would want to be alone or should I say chill with his other bitches. We made plans to stay the night together earlier that day. Later on that night, I called him just to see if our plans were still on, and he did not answer the fucking phone. I tried calling him about two more times and when he didn't answer the phone, I started calling other niggas that I really didn't want to talk to who had called me earlier that day. As I was flicking through some old text messages, Jeri's name popped up. I asked him if he wanted to come over and see me and just chill for a little while. It had been a minute since I saw him. We had talked from time to time but that was it. He seemed like he had changed so having him over don't seem so bad. Besides, it was only for one night.

Jeri responded to my text message promptly, and within twenty minutes, he was at my house.

He arrived quickly. As soon as I saw him I said, "Goddamn, motherfucker. Was you on your way before we talked?"

We laughed a little and went into the living room to watch some movies. He kept talking about us getting back together. Not trying to be funny, but I just needed some company for the night since Danger ass ain't show up. Jeri started getting on my nerves. I couldn't help it, I was so into D. Jeri had lost out; my feelings for him was gone, and I wanted D bad. I fell asleep

160

on Jeri's ass. I was a little bored with him. Plus, I was irritated with D for not showing up.

While I was sleeping, Jeri was snooping around my house, going through my cell phone and reading my text messages. He didn't like some of the text messages that he read from Richard and decided to call him up. He lied and told Richard that we got back together. He even lied and said that we'd just finished fucking. His eyes were blood shot red with a gloss to them. He was pacing back and forth, grabbing his head. He kept on yelling at me while I was laying down, sleeping. I didn't quite grasp what happened.

I just laid there staring at the ceiling. I wasn't sure how much damage he had done. All I knew was that that stunt he was pulling was the exact reason I could not fuck with him anymore. Next thing I knew, he'd put Richard on speakerphone. I could hear Richard yelling in the background to put me on the phone.

Jeri snitched and said, "She right here, yo, looking at me like she's crazy."

Richard said, "She needs to stop being a coward and just say something."

After hearing both of these bitches nagging back and forth, both of their stories was twisted, some real, some fake. I started to blurt out that I don't owe either one of them an explanation because I was single. Jeri and Richard stayed on the phone for a few minutes longer. Once they hung up, Jeri came back into the room and tried to agitate me.

I dozed off again. I wasn't listening to none of that shit. I really didn't care how either one of them felt. The way I saw it, they got back the same exact shit that they dished out to me. This time Jeri was not in charge of the situation and Jeri didn't like it. To be honest, I really couldn't understand what the fuss was about because that was my first time seeing Jeri in forever. He kept me up all night arguing, and I tried my hardest to ignore him. When it got to be too much, I asked him to leave. He stayed just as I expected, and then he snatched my cell phone.

Just as things quieted down, D called my phone. When Jeri took my phone, he turned my ringer all the way up without my knowledge. It was five-thirty in the morning. The ringing startled me. Jeri answered the phone asking Danger who he was. He didn't know because D was stored in my phone as my baby.

D blatantly told Jeri that I was his peoples, and then he asked Jeri, "Who the fuck are you?"

Jeri lied again and said, "Her boyfriend, Jerimiah."

"Yeah, nigga. I know who the fuck you is. You're that bitch-ass nigga that she broke up with because you be putting your hands on her. The only reason I'm not over there is because I fell asleep."

Seeing that D wasn't backing off made Jeri angry. He knew that meant he wasn't going to leave me alone. Jeri just would not stop the madness. He lied and told D that he just got finished fucking me.

Jeri had pissed D off to the max.

"That's not your bitch, nigga," D said. "That's our bitch."

Jeri started making threats to D, and that was the wrong move because that nigga was really 'bout that gun play. I knew the type of nigga that D was. He was a real street nigga that had been in a few shootouts. He even shot at his own dad when his dad locked him, his mom, and other siblings out of the house. It would be nothing to let Jeri see those fireworks.

I never got too see that side of D, but it was really turning me on, especially the fact he was willing to go hard and fight for me. I never meant for any of this to happen.

D said, "Let's have a party, nigga. I'm on my way."

I panicked, because D was not the type of guy to just make threats. I saw flashing lights coming from my back parking lot. It was D beeping his horn out back. He started calling my cell phone, telling me to tell Jeri to come outside. The inside of my building was fully loaded with cameras, and Danger wasn't with none of that shit because he was on them papers. He stayed and camped outside of my home for about two-and-a-half hours, waiting for Jeri to come outside. Jeri was trying to play tough for me, like he was ready to go out there. Eventually, the phone calls stop coming and the horn stopped beeping. Soon, Jeri and I were fast asleep.

I could not wait for the next morning to come so that I could get rid of Jeri's ass. My plan was to get Jeri out of my house safely and make it up to D. I had a lot of explaining to do in spite of me knowing that he fucked with other bitches. I just fucked with him so hard on the fact of him keeping it real. I never had that before. It was like a breath of fresh air. I was so used to niggas in my past relationships putting on a show. I had lucked up this time. I had finally met the man.

The next morning finally came. I woke up and saw Jeri lying next to me. I jumped up in disgust, hoping it was a nightmare. My head was throbbing like a motherfucker. I was scared to let Jeri leave, knowing Danger's capabilities. I rolled over in my bed, trying to feel for my cell phone. Once I retrieved it, I saw that I had several missed calls. Even a text message from D stating that when he caught Jeri, his ass was grass. That shit had gone way too far because of Jeri in every way possible. I had errands to run, but I was too scared to leave without Jeri because I'd shown Danger a picture of Jeri a while back when we first broke up, and now it was coming back to haunt me.

I went outside in the hallway and peeped the scene. The coast was clear. I let him walk outside by himself and told him to try not too look suspicious and to call me once he got away safely. I was hoping that D didn't remember how he looked.

I heard gunshots about five minutes after Jeri left. It was six shots, to be exact. I called Jeri's phone, but nobody answered.

By the time I arrived on the scene, Jeri was laying on the ground bleeding, and they began to put the yellow tape up. Police officers were trying to control the crowd as an EMT tried to save Jeri's life. I fell to the ground screaming once I realized Jeri had been shot. I must have passed out because I was awakened by this really strong aroma right under my nose. That's when the officers questioned me.

The first of many questions was, "Did you know the victim?"

"Yes," I responded.

"What was your relationship wlth him?"

Instead of answering, I told them that I could not answer any more questions without the presence of my attorney. The officer told me that he would be taking me to the precinct for more questioning, and that was fine.

I was nervous as a motherfucker, but that didn't matter. I still wasn't doing any talking. They put me in the police car and let me know that I was not under arrest and that it was only for questioning purposes because they had no other leads, and then they slammed the car door shut.

I asked, but they would not even tell me Jeri's status. They just took him away in the ambulance. The officer also stated that a suspicious-looking black vehicle with tinted windows was spotted driving away from the scene quickly. I had a feeling that it was D, but I wasn't talking to no cops. After I was interrogated as if I was the one who shot Jeri, Officer Valentine finally decided to let me go. Before I left, he gave me his business card and told me that if anything else came to mind, feel free to call him. We stared at each other for a brief second, and then he told me that I was free to go.

I hurried up and got my black ass out of there. It was time to figure some shit out. I had to get in contact with D and fast. I went to nearest gas station and brought a cheap phone, some shit called a Trac Fone, and called that nigga from that phone. I sent a text because I knew that he would not answer from any unknown numbers.

Hours passed by and I still hadn't gotten a response from D. I did not know how much they knew, but I had to put him down that they were on to his car. I text him again.

911/urgent.

He text me back, and I told him that we needed to talk and I wanted to meet somewhere safe. I was so scared, being in the middle of this shit. I didn't want to takes sides, and even though I hated being around Jeri, I didn't want him dead. I didn't want to go to jail, and I damn sure didn't want to get blamed for this bullshit.

My phone rang. It was D. He told me to meet him at this secret location because it was no longer safe to talk on the phone. I was paranoid. I kept thinking that he might blow my fucking head off because I knew he was involved. I was the only person that could get him put him behind bars for a long time other than Jeri, and he might have been dead. I really did not know if I should have been hooking up with him, but I put my pride aside and decided I was bringing my machete with me just in case.

While I was on my way I text Lacie and let her know I was on my way to meet D.

Once I arrived at the secret location, I looked around and D was nowhere in sight. I kept on looking around just to make sure he was not trying to set me up or some shit. Just as I began panicking, he was standing right before my eyes. I came straight out and asked him to tell me what happened.

"You already know what it is," he said.

I started crying. "What do you mean? What have you done?"

He looked at me with absolutely no emotion on his face. I was still crying as I was telling him about the officers questioning me and about them seeing his black car.

He responded, "Shhh...Don't worry, baby. The car is gone. Everything will be okay." He dug in his pocket, handed me a wad of money, and told me to lay low for a few days.

As I was walking off, he yelled, "Beauty!" and ran back over to me. He slipped something black inside of my bag. He reached for my hand and handed me a cell phone for him to call me on. He grabbed my hand and kissed it as I reached for the phone. "I love you. Wait for my call," he said.

"I'll be waiting," I said, smiling as I walked away again.

Chapter Thirty-Two

I went and grabbed me a rental, but I got it in Kim's name. I drove to Virginia and got a cheap motel and paid straight cash. I knew they would ask for I.D., so I got my homeboy to get me a few fake I.D.'s for the low. I watched TV while waiting for D to call me.

I could not believe my eyes. The Columbians came back to Richard's mom's house and slaughtered everybody. They showed a picture of Richard, his mom, and everybody else that lived there. They even killed the poor old lady. I felt sorry for them, but I was glad I left when I did. I wasn't sure if Keema knew or how much he might have told her before they came back, but I wasn't going to let her know, either.

I was all alone and bored at this dirty-ass roach motel. I had to limit who I talked to because of all that was going on. And, by me being there by myself, I started thinking about Jeri. I even blamed myself. I kept thinking that this was my fault. Even though he abused me for all of those years, he didn't deserve to die. I

169

wanted to reach out to Jeri's family to at least know his status, but me and his fam weren't on good terms, so that would have been a terrible idea. They would have sworn I had something to do with it. They probably had already given my name to the police.

I got on my knees and prayed like I never did before. As I began to stand up, I heard a loud knock at the door. I reached into my bag and got the black thing out that D put in there. I knew it would be useful. It was a black revolver. I didn't answer the door, but I had the black revolver cocked. That's when I got a text from D saying open the door.

I opened the door quickly and put the revolver away. I was puzzled; I had no idea how he'd found me in Virginia. It was strange, because I didn't tell a soul alive where I was going, but I didn't ask any questions. I was just excited to see his ass.

"The less you know, the safer you are," he said, almost as though he'd read my mind. "Beauty, you have to trust me."

I didn't know what in the hell he could have been thinking telling me that. In fact, it actually had me worried.

D started rubbing my leg as we sat on the bed. "This will all be over before you know it." D patted my leg one last time, and I got up to take a shower.

When I came out of the bathroom, there was champagne and four blunts rolled on the table. All I could smell was diesel. I looked on the bed and saw flowers, and he had his shirt off while his dick was standing tall. He kissed me on my cheek and told me that I could not take a sip until we made a toast.

"What do you want to toast to?"

"Our future."

Our glasses touched, and then we both took a few sips. That's when he told me that he was falling deeply in love with me.

"Can you keep a secret?" he asked. After I assured him that I could, he admitted to being jealous about me letting Jeri come over to my house. "Did you give my pussy away?"

"No," I whispered in his ear. I laid on the bed with my legs cocked wide open. I allowed his fingers to enter my vagina. He was a perfectionist. The way his fingers would fuck my pussy was unbelievable. He made me cum over and over again. He would hit my spot and never let it go. He had me wanting to be bad just like him— a little naughty gal. After we finished fucking. I fell fast asleep in his arms.

I woke up at seven a.m. for a bathroom run, and there was no sign of D. He left a note that said he would be contacting me soon. I hated when he would leave. I kissed the note and sighed. I didn't know what the hell I was getting myself into with this nigga, or what was about to happen next, for that matter. But I had to return soon, because I would definitely look suspicious if I didn't.

Chapter Thirty-Three

My BFF, Kim, called me to see when I was returning the rental, and she was telling me that they were hiring at the Grey Dog and that she wanted me to apply because they were looking for some new ticket agents. Kim had been working there for some years. It was a bus station. A few months back, I kept on calling her about a job. I was scared I would lose my apartment because unemployment wasn't paying me enough and I was behind on my bills. I did what my bitch told me to do and took my ass down there and filled out an application. The manager appeared to be cool as shit. His name was Raymond. He was trying to offer me a new position they were putting in place. It was called a greeter, and it was full time.

Raymond told me that I had the job and would be starting some time that following week. He was not sure on the exact day, but he said he would be definitely give me a call.

I was so excited. That was what I had been praying for. The only thing was that my old boss Deborah had copped me and one of my old

173

employees a plane ticket to Louisiana to help them out for the weekend. All expenses were paid for, even the hotel, and once we got there, we would get paid to work as well. At the last minute, I backed out because I decided I didn't want to miss out on this permanent position at the Grey Dog, and what if D needed me with all that was going on? I called Deborah up and broke the bad news to her.

She was pissed. She kept saying, "Well, I already paid for everything and I can't get a refund."

I just hung up without saying another word. I knew that she would be upset, but I had to do what was best for me. I was glad that I made that decision because Mr. Raymond ended up calling me earlier than expected.

Things were much different there than when I was a store manager. Going from being the boss and being told what to do was a big change for me, but I just went with the flow.

Upon starting, there was a big, fat, dark-skinned, blonde hair-having bitch that would be training me. Her name was Wanita. I could tell that I would not like her from the moment we met. She was just so loud and obnoxious. Kim warned me about Wanita before I even started working with her. She even told me how this bitch would tell everybody on the job how she was fucking hella bus drivers, how she would suck some of their dicks on the bus, and how whenever anybody would tell her their business, she would discuss it with everyone on the job. But the main thing she was trying to say was watch out for her. My girl Kim wasn't lying either. As soon as I met her, I could tell that bitch was scummy.

I wasn't a very sociable girl, so if you didn't know me, you would probably suspect that I was stuck up. That really was not the case at all. I just wasn't the type to get caught up with no drama at work. In my eyes, providing for my family was everything, so if I lost my job over beefing with a bitch, she was definitely going to feel it.

The very first thing that I noticed about shorty was that, while she was training me, all she would do was talk about who she fucked, how much dick she sucked, and when and where she fucked these drivers. It was sickening, because I couldn't really imagine anybody wanting to fuck this gorilla, but the worst part about it was she didn't know a damn thing about me other than my name. You know, I thought she was crazy. It appeared to me after she had given so much personal information to me about herself and she didn't receive any feedback, it caused tension. The bitch became vindictive. She started being ignorant towards me and doing things like leaving me behind the ticket counter by myself, knowing that I was still in training.

175

No Way Out

When I would ask the bitch for some help, she would huff and puff loudly in front of the drivers, exclaiming that she could not wait till she got off work. It had even gotten to the point where she wouldn't let me work a whole eight hours. It was bad enough that Raymond's ass lied. I was only a part time ticket agent and was only working three lousy days a week. I would catch a cab all the way there, and after four hours, Wanita would say I could leave. I already had so much shit on my fucking mind. I hadn't heard anything from Danger's ass in about two weeks. I knew that I would have to report my new income to unemployment, plus I was saving up that lump sum of money that D had given me towards a lawyer just in case since I still had not heard anything about Jeri.

I called a cab just before leaving the Grey Dog since the bitch was sending me home early. As soon as I got in the taxi, the driver asked me to give him directions on getting there, and I did just that. Every time I would tell the taxi driver to make a left, he would either make a right and have to turn all the way around or just completely bypass my stop and act like he didn't hear me at all. I yelled at the driver, then through the money at his ass and told him to let me the fuck out.

When I got out of the cab, it was about 9:30 at night, so it was pretty dark out. As I was walking down the street past those projects where I had previously been jumped, I saw this lady who appeared to be a fiend. She stared for a second and said that my hair was very pretty. I thanked her and started dialing my big sister's phone number. Once I walked half way down the block, the lady yelled and asked me if I minded letting her use my cell phone. Before I could say anything, she said she'd take me home for a phone call. For some reason, I didn't trust it, so I declined and kept on walking. Me and my sister was laughing about how crazy the lady sounded. Out of nowhere, this tall black dude started walking fast behind me.

My intuition told me that he was up to no good. It was like he had just snuck up on me. I started walking in the street but very close to the curb. I wanted to let him walk past me without him being too close. Once he walked past me, I sighed in relief. He was talking on his phone, anyway. I was on the phone telling my sister the description of the man just in case. Just before I finished, he got off of his phone and stood underneath a tree. I tried to run across the street, but there was too much traffic and the cars were going way too fast. I couldn't just jump in front of the cars because I would've gotten hit.

The man just grabbed me with one hand and used the other to point a tech right at my face. I was still on the phone with my sissy, holding it up using my ear and my neck. I guess my screaming made the man panic because he kept on shaking while grabbing me. My reflexes made me push him as hard as I could. That made the man angry because he threw me to the ground, and popped my purse off of my shoulders, and ran off. He didn't even attempt to take my phone.

I ran in the opposite direction like a bat out of hell, screaming at the top of my lungs for help. The whole time, I stayed on the phone with my sister, who was nine months pregnant with my niece.

This young girl saw everything and pulled right over and called the police. She signaled for me to come over and sit inside her vehicle until the police came to assist me. Luckily, the little bit of money I had on me, I had put it in my pants pocket instead of my purse. Unfortunately, my house key was in my purse, along with my learner's permit. I had just gotten it a few days before. The worst part was that my address was on it. Now, I had to live with the fear of that stupid motherfucker knowing my address and returning.

I sat in the girl's vehicle and called up the credit card company to cancel my bank cards. After I got my police report, the young girl dropped me off at my apartment building so that I could notify security to keep a look out on my house. The big wad of money was stashed inside of my apartment, so as soon as the rental office opened up my locks were changed immediately.

Since I could not get in the house that night because the robber had my keys, my sister told me to catch a cab to her house, which she would pay for, and that's what I did.

No Way Out

Chapter Thirty-Four

I was missing the shit out of D, and there was still no word from him. I decided to swing through ol' boy's hood just to see what was up. Crazy shit was none of them niggas was out, so I dialed his old phone number from one of my hot phones, and the voice on the other end of the line said, "Who dis?"

"Fuck you mean?" I asked.

"You looking for Danger?"

"You are Danger!"

"Nah, yo! Dis is his brother. Yo locked up."

"For what?" I asked.

"Yo had two attempts. The witnesses survived, and they're coming to court."

For a second D's brother sounded just like him. I was ready to be pissed. After he kept on talking, I realized that he wasn't lying. I told him to tell Danger to give me a ring.

Danger called me later that night. I was so fucking excited. I was jumping around with my boy shorts on, laughing and being silly. D surely did know how to put me in a good mood. I came out and told him about that nigga robbing me; I didn't know what else to do. I told him that I was scared to be alone. That man had violated me, and that made Danger mad. He told me not to do too much worrying and that he would be home shortly. His had his crew working 'round the clock to assure that those witnesses didn't make it to court.

Before we hung up, Danger said, "Babe, if I find out who the nigga was that robbed you, I'm going make him suffer right in front of you, so you can feel some relief."

D really had a way of making me feel good, even when things appeared to be getting rough.

He made sure he put me on his visiting list. We had so much catching up to do, because we couldn't really say what we wanted to say on those jail phones.

The very next day, I heard a knock at my door. It was his brother, Boo Boo. I was surprised, I might say, but I didn't ask any questions at all. I just opened the door with a puzzled look on my face.

He was holding a plastic bag with a shoe box inside of it. He handed it to me and told me to sit down and open it. Once it was open, I couldn't believe my eyes. Danger told his brother to give me another gun for protection, and that I should carry it at all times. Boo Boo cleaned it well and handed me a brand-new box of bullets.

Melanie Forbes
As he was leaving, he gave me a five. In his hand was a stack of money with nothing but one hundred dollar bills, which he put into my hand.

No Way Out

Chapter Thirty-Five

After the robbery, I decided that I wasn't going back to work at the Grey Dog anymore. It was too much drama, and I blamed that bitch Wanita for me getting robbed in the first place. If it wasn't for her sending me home so early, it never would have happened, and she only did it because she didn't like me.

I was scheduled to go back to work the following day, but I decided not to go in, or even call, for that matter, 'cause me seeing Wanita would have caused her to get an ass whipping.

After I missed two days in a row without anyone hearing from me, their company's accountant called me. Her name was Sally. She wanted to know if everything was okay. I came out and told the truth about how I planned on resigning because I didn't like how Wanita was treating me and how, when I would work with her, my drawer would be short sometimes because she was stealing the money. Five minutes later, Raymond called. We talked for about an hour, and he told me that he'd set everything straight and wanted me to join the team again. I accepted, even though I was a little hesitant at first.

A few days later at work, all the top dogs at the company had come down. Word was going around that the employees were not being treated fairly, so they were trying to form a union. That's why corporate had come down. Grey Dog didn't want their Baltimore location to become a union like a few of their other locations had done. They needed to maintain control and power.

Corporate walked around and spoke to all of the employees who seemed to be creating all of the static in the building. Wanita's name was written all over it. After pampering all of the employees enough to convince us not to go through with forming the union, corporate decided that they would no longer be needing Wanita's services. Besides, she caused so many problems amongst other employees that it was time for that hoe to go.

When Raymond was told that he would be the one doing the dirty work, he was furious. He broke down crying in front of one of the bus driver's. Word was going around that Raymond and Wanita maintained a sexual relationship, and he was scared that she would put his job and relationship on the line. He had a long-term girlfriend that he was with before his employment with the company. Him and Michelle use to be crack addicts before someone came along and helped them get off of drugs. They started out as janitors. Soon after, they both were promoted to managers. She stayed in D.C., and he moved to Baltimore. So, he didn't need Wanita messing things up for him, and he didn't want his girl knowing anything about him fucking Wanita.

No Way Out

Chapter Thirty-Six

Today was the big day. I was going to visit Danger. His mom Sydney, was picking me up from my house. On our way to the jail, she stopped up the street and went on the strip to get some weed. She was exactly like her son. She carried a bunch of cigarillos around at a time. The niggas from the street walked up to the car, and she asked them where the diesel was at.

I was laughing my ass off inside. I could not believe that his mom was just like us. She rolled the window back up and asked me if I was smoking. I wasn't quite sure if that was a trick question or not, but my habit was calling, and I decided to join her. On the way to the detention center, we got high as a bitch.

Once we arrived at the jail, the line was long as shit. This bitch was cursing the fucking C.O. out. Then, she got out of the line and called someone from her cell phone. She was yelling and screaming to the person on the phone that he better not have had a visit from another bitch.

189

She continued carrying on until they called the police and forced her off of the property.

After getting patted down like we were some straight up criminals, we were on our way up to visit Danger. He gave me a big smile, and his gold teeth lit up the room. It was like the streets up in that motherfucker to him because every nigga that walked past him, he either knew or they were giving him dap. He was popular everywhere he went.

I let him talk to Mrs. Sydney first. I just stood on the side and gave them a chance to talk alone. Once they were finished, I sat down, and he started explaining to me how he got caught up in those attempts he was facing. He said his ex-girl, who he had just denied a visit from, started fucking this nigga he was beefing with. The dude's people tried to kill a man, and his girl and Danger's ex-girl were in the room, hiding in the closet. They did not know she was still in the house. Once they started shooting, she ran. They caught her and pistol whipped her really bad and told her they would kill her if she didn't go to the police and say it was Danger. She went down to the precinct and told them she wanted to be a witness to two attempted murders. Shorty went so hard that she convinced the victims to go along with it, and told them if they didn't, there would be consequences.

His mom came back over and squeezed her skinny ass on the bench with me. Danger told Mrs. Sydney that, when he came home, me and him were going to make a baby. She just smiled and patted me on the back.

She then looked at Danger and said, "Son, promise me you're going to come home and do her right, because I know how you are."

"Mom, I'm come home and do her right," he said. "I'll get a lil job, stay out of trouble, and start a family with her."

She smiled again. "I hope so."

I could not believe that Danger was actually saying we were together and he wanted a family with me.

We all sat around chatting for a little while longer. Eventually, a big fat C.O. bitch said that our visit was over. That made Danger mad. Mrs. Sydney told Danger that we had to leave and that we loved him very much. She also told him to call us later on.

He yelled loudly, "Fuck that fat bitch! I'm not going nowhere. I hate this shit. They're going to put on me on lock down, 'cause I'm going throw piss and shit on her fat ass once I get to my cell!"

Everyone else had left the visiting room, but Danger did not want to leave. His eyes had watered up, which made me sad. The C.O. had come back over too see what the holdup was. She wanted to know why Danger still had visitors. As she was coming toward us, we were saying our goodbyes. Danger resisted, and the guard used force. D almost fell out of the chair when she grabbed him. He got so mad that he spit in her face. He got up and kicked her on the floor. Me and his mom stood helpless on the other side, begging him to stop. It was like he didn't hear us. He would not stop for nothing. All of a sudden, lots of guards came running in from every direction.

They were jumping on Danger, beating him with nightsticks and mace, and one officer even tasered him.

His mom yelled, "Stop! This is against the law!"

We gave each other a big hug to block ourselves from seeing it and to give each other some comfort. After a few minutes, Danger was no longer fighting, or even making any noise, for that matter! There was blood everywhere. I kept crying while calling his name, but he wouldn't respond.

His mom began yelling, "All of you motherfuckers are going to pay for what you did too my son!"

We knew he had to be unconscious. At least ten guards had been beating him.

A guard came to the door and escorted us out of the jail.

Mrs. Sydney called me a few days later and said that Danger was sent out to the hospital.

But the good news was that he was okay. He sustained only mild injuries: a broken arm and just some minor cuts and bruises. The night that they beat him, he had a seizure and a broken rib, so they had to keep him for further observation and testing.

"Now, for the bad news," she said.

"Lay it on me," I replied.

"No one can visit him in the hospital because he is still a ward of the state and they have him handcuffed to the hospital bed."

No Way Out

Chapter Thirty-Seven

Danger's little brother and I were catching up on some shit, and he kept me company since he knew that I was down and out from missing his big brother and all. We left to go to the bar, and as we were walking, a red S.U.V with tinted windows slowed down and drove past. We really didn't pay it much attention because we were high as fuck. We went inside the bar and ordered our drinks as planned.

On our way back to my house, we noticed the same S.U.V had circled the block and stopped midway in the block as we hesitantly walked past. All four windows quickly went down, and that's when Boo Boo yanked me down by my shirt and pulled me to the ground. Next thing I know, bullets were flying everywhere. I could see them flying past me. We used the parked car as a shield. Lord knows I tried my hardest not to look up.

Boo Boo whispered to me, "On the count of three, run. I will cover you."

We both knew that, if they really wanted us dead, they would probably be getting out of the

195

car to make sure that the job was finished. He pulled out his fully-loaded gun and helped me up, and I ran with my head down. He let me get a little bit ahead of him while he staggered behind, trying his best to protect me. I kept on looking back. He was yelling for me to run. He was doing a good job shooting, but two of them got out of the car.

Boo Boo started yelling, "Ah, shit! Beauty, just run. Don't look back. I will cover you."

I ran over to him and took his gun and started shooting at those niggas. I did not want to do it, but I had to if I wanted to live. I had to suck that scared shit up. I hit one of 'em, or something must have happened, because the gunshots stopped and the S.U.V had disappeared.

We ran as fast as we could to an abandoned house. It was pretty difficult for us to run with Boo Boo limping and all. The vacant house had a broken window. I climbed right on in and let Boo Boo in through the front door. There was a long trail of blood following Boo Boo. I helped him to sit down. I really didn't know what to do, so I ripped my shirt off and used it to apply pressure to the gunshot wound on his leg.

He was in so much pain and losing a lot of blood, but that did not stop him from staring at me. He was looking at my big breasts. I guess it was hard not to watch them being that he could see my bra.

He began sweating. He could tell I was getting a little nervous, so he began to direct me on what to do. He told me to get the liquor that we had bought from the bar and pour some on his leg. I did exactly what he said, but it didn't appear to be working.

He kept on yelling and screaming, "Fuck, fuck, fuck! Beauty, come here."

I did as he said.

"Just in case I don't make it, thanks for everything." He kissed my lips.

I knew it was wrong, but I kind of liked it. I could not just let him die. I had to think of something. "Yo, Boo," I said, "You have to go the fucking hospital!"

He refused and asked me if I had any serious beef with anyone. I told him that I didn't and that I was going to ask him the same thing.

He said, "Once I put money out on the streets, niggas going to start talking."

After the pain meds and alcohol wore off, he laid all the way down. I kept calling out his name, but he would not move. He was going in and out of consciousness. He was definitely fading away because of how much blood he had lost. He was dying. I started kicking him and telling him to wake up, but he just would not respond. I poured the last little bit of alcohol left on his leg, and he would not budge. I was shaking and crying. The last resort was calling Mrs. Sydney, and that's what I did. When I called her and told her what had happened, she was frantic but she gave me Danger's social security number so that Boo Boo could pose as him at the hospital. Boo Boo was on parole and had no more chances left. I hurried up and poured a whole bunch of water on Boo Boo's face. Once he regained consciousness, I rushed him to the hospital, where he was admitted under Danger's name.

Once we arrived at the hospital with the little energy he had left, I helped him out of the car and called the hospital from a payphone and said there was a guy laying on the ground outside the building. I sat in my car close by, patiently waiting for them to come outside to aide him before I left. Shit was getting crazy. Somebody had it out for us, and I had no idea what was going on. One thing I did know was that the only way to find answers would be too get in contact with Danger, but that was going to be a hard task since he was on high security at the hospital and would be on lock down once he got back to the jail.

I felt so sorry for Mrs. Sydney. She had just buried Danger and Boo Boo's older brother only a few years before. He was a big-time drug dealer that was very respected, but he had gotten shot up and killed in the middle of the block that they lived on. After hearing several gunshots, she ran outside only to find out that it was her son, Kevin, dead in the middle of the street. The police never found any suspects, and it became a cold case. They lived in a rough part of town, and around there, even if somebody saw anything, they wouldn't say anything. That came with living in the streets of Baltimore city. In order to survive, everyone knew that silence was the key, and there was always a hothead around willing to shut someone up.

She said she still remembered his face as he laid there on the ground, dead. If that poor lady lost another son, she probably wouldn't make it. I called back to let her know that he made it to the hospital and that I didn't know his status.

She began crying and told me that she would call if she heard anything.

I said okay and hung up. I was at a loss for words, too. Both of her sons were in the hospital at the same damn time, and there was absolutely nothing that she could do about it.

No Way Out

Chapter Thirty-Eight

I was trying to clear my head and all. I needed a break, for sure. Everywhere I turned, there was death or people seriously getting hurt, and I was always around to witness it.

I missed my girl. I had to get up with my bitch, Lacie. She'd finally had her little baby boy. We were so close you would have thought I was her baby's father. It seemed like she was pregnant forever, and I didn't even get the chance to see the baby. It was like she was ducking me out or some shit. Ever since the Jeri situation, every time I would call her, the calls would be brief. Half of the time, she wouldn't even respond to my text messages, and she stayed with her phone in her hand. That was not like her at all.

I felt like she was blaming me for what happened to Jeri. I felt bad about what happened to him, but truth is, he didn't know when to shut the fuck up, and it finally caught up with him. She used to be my bitch, my ride or die, the one I did all of my dirty work with. Now, I was going through all of this shit alone with no

201

one to vent to. This wasn't the type of shit I could just randomly call somebody up and talk about. If I told the wrong person, it could compromise their safety, so I had to be mindful of that. Plus, I didn't know where her head was at, so it was time to give her ass a surprise visit at her house. I was going to make her look me right in the eyes so that I could find out what really happened to Jeri.

I parked down the street from her house in a burgundy rental car and walked to her door. I knocked on the hollow door and no one answered, but I had the strangest feeling that someone was right inside, because I could feel them watching me. After knocking several times and getting no response, I walked back to the car and sat and watched her house from there.

I sat for several hours and, still, no Lacie. As I was turning the radio on and putting the van in drive, Lacie and her mom were leaving their house. I quickly threw the car back into park and jumped right out. I walked over to them and made a little small talk, made up a story about me already being in the neighborhood, and said I needed to use their bathroom very badly.

They both gave each other a crazy look, as if to say it wasn't a good idea or something.

"The toilet is stopped up. Plus, the house is nasty," Lacie's mom said. "I wouldn't want you to tell anybody that out house is a mess, and I'd be embarrassed for you to see it."

"No worries. I'm only doing a number one," I said, laughing. "Besides, we're like family. I don't care how your house looks."

Before she could get her keys out to lock up, I forced my way inside of their house. I was going to give Lacie no other choice but to talk to me, even if we had to fight.

That's when they gave in and followed me inside. As soon as I looked up, I saw him there. He was lying on the mattress, all bandaged up, in the middle of the living room. There were a few oxygen tanks and a wheel chair. Shocked, I just stood there crying. He must have heard my voice, because he opened up his eyes and tried to sit up. I ran over to him.

It was Jeri. He wasn't dead.

No Way Out

Chapter Thirty-Nine

He was calling out to me. He tried to speak but his words were muffled. All I could hear was a bunch of muttering. I grabbed his hand tight and said, "Shhh, it's okay; everything is going to be okay."

He kept trying to tell me something, but I wouldn't allow him to. He needed his rest and that was all I really cared about, so that was exactly what he was going to do.

Not even paying attention, I didn't realize that there was a police officer slumped over in the chair. I had to get the fuck out of there before he realized who I was and start questioning me about my relationship with Jeri and connection to his attempted murder. I could not believe that they had Jeri in police protection because they figured whoever started to kill him would come back for sure if they found out Jeri was still alive. That would explain why Lacie was avoiding me.

As I was walking out of the door, Lacie whispered, "I will explain later."

As she was closing the door, I could hear the officer yelling, "Wait, come back!"

I ran as fast I could to my car and got the hell out of there.

My nervous ass was backing into cars, and I even ran into the curb. I almost hit a woman and her child. I was so scared that I could not stop shaking. Seeing Jeri like that really fucked me up in the head. I didn't even apologize to them. It was clear that that poor woman was frightened. I was less than a half inch away from probably killing them. The lady ran off with her baby in her arms. My crazy ass just sat there in a daze thinking about how Jeri had the look of death upon him. I felt like giving up. I could not help but wonder in which direction the police were going with their investigation and how much they really knew about what had happened.

Chapter Forty

I went back to work and continued on as if everything was normal. But, first, I had to get rid of that rental car; I did not need anyone on my trail. I wasn't sure if anybody got my tag numbers, so I was just going to remain on the safe side.

First day back at the Grey Dog, I was called into the supervisor's office to go over my new schedule on the weekends. Bethea said that me and Ashton would have rotating schedules on the weekends. But Ashton was not trying to hear none of that shit. In fact, she did not want to work any weekends at all. The fucked-up part about it was that the bitch had just come back from maternity leave. We got hired at the same damn time. Her cousin, Marsha, got her in and my bestie, Kim, got me in. But when Ashton first got hired, she was already pregnant and kept her pregnancy a secret. Once she got to about six or seven months, she went into labor early and had no other choice but to confess about her pregnancy.

Meanwhile, I was left to work every weekend. Plus, I was working the evening shift, so you know I was a mad motherfucker. For her to come back to work on some ignorant shit and tell the supervisor to change her schedule because she not working any weekends and that they are going to have to make me do the weekends definitely caused some friction between us. Bethea did the best that she could to be fair without having too many run ins with Mr. Raymond.

Mr. Raymond was not as nice as I thought. He did whatever he could to favor the cousins. Not too long after that, they hired this boney-ass bitch named Blonelle. This bitch had so much weave in her hair, you would have thought that she'd robbed a horse. Mr. Raymond would always call me Beauty, because he saw it tatted on my wrist. The bitch would get jealous and talk shit about me to Mr. Raymond. She had a big-ass gap in her teeth and had the nerve to always have her mouth in everything, stirring up a whole bunch of shit. She was Ashton's best friend.

At first, Marsha was cool as shit. We worked on the same shift, and she would show me the ropes because I was still a newbie. But once Marsha got pregnant and her baby's father got killed, home girl changed. She did a whole one-eighty on me. Her, her cousin Ash, and Blonelle would walk around the job starting shit and saying all kinds of ignorant shit to the employees that they did not hang wit. Raymond's ass would let them do anything they wanted, from calling out, to no call no shows, to cursing customers out, stealing on camera, and blatantly disrespecting other coworkers. It was even to the point that he would not care if all three of them would call out on the same shift and he would have to cover it and come to the front desk to sell tickets.

Mr. Raymond was so caught up that they made him look like a fool in front of his bosses. He played both sides of the fence. He would tell me all the bad shit they would say about me and entertain them when they would talk about me the whole time. The truth is that he was only mad because he wanted to fuck me and I was not having that shit. To be spiteful, he started doing shit like letting Ashton have every weekend off. Next, he promoted Marsha to a higher position without even posting the position because he did not want anyone else to apply for that position.

No Way Out

Chapter Forty-One

I came home from work with a lot on my brain. I couldn't take any more bullshit, and that meant from anybody. How foolish of me for thinking that I could advance at the Grey Dog. I was pacing back and forth, staring at my white walls— a bitch was going crazy.

Just when I was about to break down and cry, a strange number called my house phone. I was a bit hesitant to answer it, but, to my surprise, it was my baby, Danger. We hadn't talked in a minute. I mean, I knew what he was dealing with, but I was still feeling neglected. I wanted to tell him everything that I was dealing with, but I didn't want to overwhelm him. I could hear in his voice that something was wrong.

He started crying really hard. At that moment, I knew it was bad.

"Mariah," he said, "Boo Boo is gone. They killed my little nigga. What the fuck am I going to do?"

I threw the phone down in disbelief and fell to the ground, crying and screaming, "No!" Boo Boo looked after me and tried to hold me down

211

because Danger couldn't. Who was going to be there now? It seemed like every time I got close to someone, they'd leave me or die.

I wiped my eyes and picked the phone up.

That's when Danger said, "Whoever killed my brother is going to die straight like that," I said, "Come on Danger quit playing around," which was sort of like a code, reminding him that he was being recorded on the jail phone. But he didn't seem too care, anyway. There wasn't too much Danger cared about, and with Boo Boo gone, I knew the streets weren't going to be safe anymore.

Mrs. Sydney was in charge of making the funeral arrangements for her son. It was a sad day for the entire family. Even though Boo Boo was in the streets, he was loved by many, and he showed the same love back. The only way you didn't like him was if you were jealous of him or hated Danger, who had lots of enemies. It was possible that someone could have killed Boo Boo to get back at Danger. The hardest part was Mrs. Sydney losing a second child. It was devastating.

Danger was trying to see if the judge would allow him to come to the funeral to see his brother laid to rest. The funeral was going to be seven days from the day that Boo Boo was killed. The courts allowed Danger some kind of temporary release from jail so that he could attend the funeral. He was being released two days before the funeral, and they made it perfectly clear that, if he tried any shaky shit or was even a minute late coming back, they were going to add an additional fifteen years to his prison sentence, even though he still didn't know how much time he was going to get in the first place since he hadn't been convicted of any crime. But the time they were trying to charge him with was sick.

He was lucky. My nigga had no restrictions other than to be back to the jail no later than five days after the funeral. I couldn't believe that, after he left Mrs. Sydney's, he came straight to my house. As soon as I opened the door, he pulled me close and hugged me while asking what he was going to do.

All I could do was rub his back, because I had no words of consolation. I mean, the nigga was with me when he got shot. All I could remember was the nigga losing consciousness and me being scared. The hospital told his mom that Boo Boo lost too much blood and died on the surgery table. Even talking about it made Danger sick to his stomach.

No Way Out

Chapter Forty-Two

It was a very large funeral. All the realest niggas from the city were in there. Even gang members attended it. I saw black, red, and blue blending in with the crowd. I had the honor of sitting right next to Mrs. Sydney and my baby, Danger, because I was going be there to help my man get through this, and that was all I knew.

Walking up to view his body was crucial. Danger couldn't seem to take his eyes off his baby bro. Danger watched as everybody went up to view his brother's body. In his eyes, everyone was a suspect. I even wondered if he thought I might have had something to do with it since I was there when it happened. But he kept on grilling everyone, even some family members. He just did not know anymore.

There was this one guy who went up to view the body. He didn't look familiar at all. He went to view Boo Boo's body for a quick sec, and then he turned around and quickly exited the door.

As the dude was leaving, Danger whispered in my ear, "I will be right back."

After about ten minutes, he returned, and everyone was leaving to go to the repass. A few of us stopped to talk as we were about to get inside of our cars, and an old lady that cleaned up the church ran outside of the building screaming at the top of her lungs, "Help! Somebody, help, please! She's dying!"

A flock of people quickly ran back inside of the church behind the lady, only to find a six-year-old, little girl lying helplessly on the bathroom floor. It looked like a horror movie. The poor baby was coughing and spitting up blood. Her whole body was covered in blood. Danger's uncle, Sammy, who was an ex-marine, took off his shirt and used it to apply pressure to the little girl's neck. She had already lost a lot of blood; she was running out of time.

"The man," she said.

It sounded as if she was trying to let us know that a man had hurt her. I felt so bad for her; she was only a child. Who in the hell could hurt her? She was a fucking baby, for God's sake.

I got on my knees and prayed with her and promised her that everything would be okay. I was holding the little girl tightly while rocking her back and forth. I could feel her lifeless body fading away. That was only my second time seeing baby girl. Maybe even my last. She kept

216

on trying to speak. I couldn't quite hear her because her words were muffled, but I did hear her say that she was cold. She continued trying to talk while coughing up blood.

I put my hand on top of her mouth. "Shhh, baby girl. Don't worry. It will be okay," I said with tears running down my neck. I was so scared for her, I just couldn't help but to keep reassuring her that everything was all good. But deep in my heart, I did not feel that way. I didn't want her to be scared to die. EMS were on their way, but it seemed like they were taking forever.

She came to the funeral with Mrs. Sydney because her mom couldn't attend it. She had to work and they would not allow her the day off, because he wasn't immediate family. Plus, she was a single mother of three. But baby Taylor loved herself some Boo Boo, so her mom allowed her to come. She'd had to use the rest room, so they allowed her to use it alone since it was only family and friends attending the funeral. Some sick fuck had slit baby Taylor's throat and left her in the stall to die alone.

Mrs. Syd was so out of it that she did not even notice that baby Taylor was missing. She got out of the car once the ambulance had arrived to see what was going on. She had been sitting in the car the entire time waiting for everybody to go to the repass together. She followed EMS back inside the church, asking what was going on.

No Way Out

Chapter Forty-Three

My mind was racing. Everything seemed to have been going wrong. My life was in shambles. Lacie used to fuck with Boo Boo a little something; she'd met him through Danger. Danger and Boo Boo were as thick as thieves, so you wouldn't see one without the other too often. Every time I would go to see Danger, she would kick it with Boo. But ever since all of that shit with Jeri, we hadn't spoken. I was so fucked up inside that I couldn't reach out to her. Even though they weren't in a serious relationship, that was her little boo. Personally, I didn't think she took him seriously, because she was digging his cousin, Insane, and that's when they started, too.

She liked Boo Boo because he was a chill little nigga, and he wasn't disrespectful. Truth is, he wanted to be just his big brother, and he was not flashy enough for her. Yo really just started jumping off the porch for real. On the other hand, Insane's crazy ass was just the opposite. He had lots of bitches, he was very disrespectful and flashy, he had a few cars and chains, and would kill a nigga on the spot if he had to, and Lacie loved his swag along with the fact he was so crazy.

Both cousins new what it was with Lacie. They decided to keep it in the family. They competed with each other a little bit, but nothing more than that. I think they all enjoyed their little love triangle.

As my frustration grew, it caused me to go home and drink and drink and drink until I couldn't drink any more. I was watching Maury while sitting on the sofa, laughing so hard. I thought it was funny that these bitches thought they knew who their baby daddies were, and they would have to test like five men. Next thing you know, I was out like a light.

All of a sudden, I heard voices, but my head was spinning. I couldn't tell if I was imagining shit or not. The voices were deep and loud. Every time I would open my eyes, a bright light seemed to be shining on them, and it would hurt my eyes. I really thought that I was dreaming, but I wasn't. Finally able to open my eyes some, I saw four white men staring me in my face.

I screamed as loud as I could. One of the guys had a rag, and another one had a needle. Two of the guys held me down. The fat one put the rag over my nose while another one stuck me with the needle. I could feel my insides burning, and that's when I went out.

After a while, I began to wake up out of it. My head was spinning, and I felt dizzy. My head was banging on something that felt like the floor. They had covered up my eyes. It was so dark and scary. They even had my hands tied behind my back, but, surprisingly, my feet were loose.

All of a sudden, we came to a stop. I heard the same four men. They got out of the car and slammed the doors. I could hear the voices coming closer and closer toward me. I balled up as tight as I could. Even with the blindfold, I could see some lights pointed directly in my face. I heard another door open, and I asked, "What you want?"

One of the men laughed and said, "It is your lucky day. You're a special delivery. Lucky girl." He then licked my face as if I was an animal. The man placed my feet on the ground, untied my hands all rough, and then guided me in the direction he wanted me to go. Next, he pushed me in the back of my head and said, "Enjoy."

No Way Out

Chapter Forty-Four

I took the blindfold off and began to walk around, staring at the beautiful house, with beautiful wall paintings. I was beyond impressed. The house was a mansion. I could have never even dreamed of something this beautiful. I was clueless. I just could not seem to grasp what I could have done to get kidnapped then dropped off at this beautiful house, which appeared to be empty. I walked around, searching for answers and screaming, "Hello? Is anyone there?"

My wrists were still sore from being tied up. While walking around, I couldn't help but notice champagne and wine glasses and dinner for two. I crept upstairs and walked past the bathroom, where I saw rose petals all over the floor leading up to the Jacuzzi. It was so romantic. I also found a beautiful red gown with red stiletto pumps. I walked up to get a closer view, and there was a note taped to the mirror, saying *get in*. I was a tad bit nervous at first, not knowing who in the hell wanted me in this house to begin with. For a second, I thought, *what a beautiful way to die!* I giggled to myself, took my clothes off as fast as I could, and jumped inside of the hot tub.

This was not your ordinary Jacuzzi, or bathroom, for that matter. The Jacuzzi was the size of an outside pool. A scented aroma filled the air. I decided to loosen up and take a swim. As I was coming back up from under the water, somebody grabbed me from behind, forcefully pulling me out of the water. I tried to pull away, but gravity would not allow me to. As I was turning around, he pulled me closer to him and started caressing my breasts. For some reason, he had a way with my nipples. I wanted it so bad even though I knew it was wrong.

I yelled, "Jeri, stop!"

I couldn't believe what the fuck I was saying. It was Jeri. I cried for joy and laughed at the same time. I was so happy he was okay. I hated this man so much for all of the shit he'd put me through. I never thought I would be so happy to see him.

He lifted me up in the air as high as he could, spun me all around, and gave me a big kiss on the lips. Next, he carried me out of the water and told me to get dressed. I put on the red gown and pumps that were laid out for me. While getting dressed, I couldn't help but wonder what the fuck was going on. I didn't even bother doing anything to my hair other than patting it dry with the towel. I had that pretty shit once it was wet. It curled up, so I just put on the matching red MAC lipstick that I had to go with the rest of my outfit and kept it moving.

There were just too many steps to walk down. They were marble, at that, so it made them slippery. It was difficult, trying to walk down all of those steps with my long, skimpy, tight-fitting dress and stilettos, especially since the staircase was a spiral one.

Jeri met me at the bottom of the steps. He greeted me with a kiss, swept me off of my feet, and he carried me to the table. The setup was extravagant. I mean, candles were lit everywhere. Our entrée consisted of lobster tails, fresh string beans seasoned with garlic sauce, filet mignon, and mashed potatoes with butter and chives, along with some Moet. Dinner was grand, and Jeri knew that seafood held the key to my heart. Surprisingly, he had remembered after all of that time.

He kept talking and talking about a whole bunch of nothing, but I wanted to know why I was here. I mean, I missed him and all, but the last time I saw him, he was in police protection, breathing through oxygen tanks, and the time before that, I thought he'd died. Yet, he'd had me kidnapped and brought to a mansion. This would be a beautiful place, that nobody knew about, to kill me and leave my body.

I couldn't hold it in any longer. As he was reaching his arm out to pass me some dessert, I stood up and said, "Jeri, I need answers now." I took the last sip of my drink and folded my arms.

Jeri ran over to me and said, "Babe, I'm only trying to protect you"

"From what when you have been the one hurting me the whole time? It's time for me to go." I took the heels off and ran upstairs to get the clothes I'd arrived in. After running up all of those stairs, my legs were tired.

I had to find somewhere to sit. That shit had me out of breath. I couldn't seem to find the bathroom, but I stumbled across a bedroom that had fourteen karat gold plated on the dressers and headboard. The blanket was all black fur, and he had it covered in red rose petals. A part of me wanted to stay. It was so cozy. I was only playing myself. I had no money on me, no idea where I was, and, plus, that drink was beginning to catch up with me. That left me no choice but to stay the night because it was too late to leave even if I wanted to. I was so gone off the Moet that once I laid on my stomach, I was fast asleep.

I could feel my dress rising up, but I was too intoxicated to move. I felt my panties move to the side, followed by some lips sucking on my pussy. I kept muttering, "Stop," but I was too weak and drunk to move. I could feel Jeri pouring warm champagne on my back, and then he licked it off. Even more sexual than normal, he began licking chocolate strawberries off of my nipples.

I woke up the next morning feeling around the bed for Jeri. I had a nasty headache from the night before. I called out to his ass several times. I needed him to get me an aspirin, but he never responded. I went back to sleep, assuming he was cooking me breakfast or something in the mansion.

A few hours later, I woke back up and looked at my cell phone. The liquor must have worn off. I was in my house, on the sofa, in the same damn spot I fell asleep in. I was irritated as shit after realizing that that was nothing more than a fucking dream.

No Way Out

Chapter Forty-Five

I went around the way just to check up on Mrs. Sydney, and, boy, did it bring back so many memories of Danger and Boo. I thought it would make her happy, so I surprised her. I wanted her to know I would be there for her. I stopped at the gas station first for some cigarillos and got her some stuff shrimp from Moe's. Before I left, I called Danger up to see if he wanted something 'cause that nigga loved himself some seafood, but he never answered the phone. I didn't know what the fuck was going on with his ass, because I hadn't heard from him since the funeral. I guess Danger was back on his hoe shit. Maybe he had to fuck him a hoe or two before he turned himself in.

After finally arriving on the block, I ran into his cousin, Insane, and copped some grass from him. I asked him if he'd spoken to Danger, and he said that he hadn't seen that nigga, either. I figured that he was just trying to cover up for his cousin. I don't know why I even asked him, anyway. That nigga was acting a little strange.

Maybe I was just overreacting, but I didn't get a good vibe from him at all.

I put my little shit up in my dip, grabbed our food, and got out of the car. I saw candles and balloons, and everyone was standing around with their T-shirts on that said "R.I.P."

I decided to walk over and join the fam. I got a quick glance at one of the shirts and saw a picture of Baby Taylor with the words 'rest in peace.' They were having a candlelight vigil for Boo Boo and Baby Taylor. There was so much shit going on. I felt so sorry for their family.

Danger was nowhere in sight, and Insane was right up the street slinging and didn't even attend the candle light vigil for his cousins. Nobody at the vigil had heard or seen Danger in a few days. All I could do was pray that he was somewhere safe, because my gut was telling me that something wasn't right. Especially when he didn't show up for the candlelight vigil!

www.ingramcontent.com/pod-product-compliance
Lightning Source LLC
Chambersburg PA
CBHW060427180626
46817CB00007B/2703